He touched her cheek with his fingers,
then pulled her up to him. They kissed
long and deliberately until finally she
broke away from him, like a swimmer
exploding through the surface for air.

She slid down to the floor before him.
She drew him out and then bowed over
him. After a minute, she rode back onto
her heels and shrugged her blouse off her
shoulders.

She rested her head on the top of his
knee. "I'll do anything for you, Winn
Cahill. Anything you want."

**All Cahill wants is more love, more sex.
But Liana's price is the most deadly
desire of the human heart . . .**

BLIND OBSESSION

BLIND OBSESSION

K. Patrick Conner

A SIGNET BOOK

SIGNET
Published by the Penguin Group
Penguin Books USA Inc., 375 Hudson Street,
New York, New York 10014, U.S.A.
Penguin Books Ltd, 27 Wrights Lane,
London W8 5TZ, England
Penguin Books Australia Ltd, Ringwood,
Victoria, Australia
Penguin Books Canada Ltd, 10 Alcorn Avenue,
Toronto, Ontario, Canada M4V 3B2
Penguin Books (N.Z.) Ltd, 182-190 Wairau Road,
Auckland 10, New Zealand

Penguin Books Ltd, Registered Offices:
Harmondsworth, Middlesex, England

Published by Signet, an imprint of New American Library, a division
of Penguin Books USA Inc. This is an authorized reprint of a hard-
cover edition published under the title *Kingdom Road* by Donald I.
Fine, Inc.

First Signet Printing, November, 1992
10 9 8 7 6 5 4 3 2 1

for Christine

They have sown the wind,
and they shall reap the whirlwind.

HOSEA 8:7

CHAPTER 1

HE SPOTTED HER purely by chance—a sudden glimpse that caught his eye like a ray of light. Her long, blond hair was drawn back into a single, thick braid. A silver earring flashed along the side of her neck.

She cut through the murky blue light, skirting the dance floor. Even from across the club, Cahill knew it was her. Her threadbare blue jeans slid down into black leather boots. Beneath her calfskin vest, the white shirt knotted across her stomach might even have been his own.

His heart raced. He was afraid to take his eyes off her. He stepped up to the edge of the stage to get a better look, but then she vanished, disappearing into the dark shadows near the bar.

He couldn't wait for Steele to bring the song to an end. He jerked the cord jack out of his Stratocaster, dropped the guitar into its case, then plunged off the front of the stage in pursuit of her.

He fought his way across the Wishing Well.

Smoke marbled the stale air. Shafts of blue and red light angled down from the lamps mounted on the ceiling. Seized by panic, he stopped and spun around. He'd lost her. As suddenly as she'd walked back into his life, she was gone.

But then he glimpsed her again, down a dark hallway. He rushed after her, fighting through the mob pressing up to the bar, his lodestar the green exit sign above the door at the back of the club. He cut in front of a waitress in a black leather skirt and fishnet stockings. Suddenly a forearm caught him in the chest. The blow straightened him up. Planted in front of him was a thick, heavyset man in an army fatigue jacket. Before he could say anything, Cahill raised both hands in apology and surrender, then dodged past him down the hall.

Again she'd disappeared, but this time he knew where she was.

He crashed through the bathroom door. Two women were leaning into a mirror ringed by burned-out light bulbs. In the iridescent glass one was inspecting her thick, crusted eyelashes, the other drawing her mouth in red lipstick. They gasped, then shrank back against each other.

Cahill pounded on the door of the first stall. When it crashed back against the wall, he moved on to the next, but she wasn't there either. He worked quickly down the row of stalls, banging the doors open until he knew she had to be in the last one.

He reached down and tried the latch.

"What do you want?" she shouted.

He kicked the door with the heel of his boot, but it didn't give. He stepped back, then threw his shoulder into it, and the latch gave out beneath him.

The door swung back into her knees. She screamed, clutching her hands between her legs, then doubling over to cover herself. Her shrill voice split the perfumed air.

As she lifted her head to look at him, he realized he'd made a terrible mistake. Her face was pinched and narrow, her eyes green and set close together. He'd never seen her before in his life.

A hand clamped down on his shoulder. Steele spun him around.

"What the hell are you doing?" demanded Steele, but didn't wait for an explanation.

He grabbed Cahill's arm and dragged him toward the door. As he shoved him into the hall, Steele turned back to the women at the mirror, his boyish cheeks dimpling as he smiled.

"As you were, ladies," he said. "I hope you'll forgive the interruption."

He pushed Cahill out through the exit, into the alley that ran behind the club. Above the door, the name of the Wishing Well was written in sections of white neon lariat. Steele paced through the flickering light.

"You want to tell me what the fuck is going on?" he shouted.

"It was a simple mistake," Cahill said.

Steele hurled a beer bottle down the alley. It shattered high against a brick wall, the glass raining down onto a dumpster bin. Rats scattered out from beneath it.

"You jump down off the stage in the middle of a set, you chase some woman into the can and then all but drag her out of a stall, and you call it a simple mistake?"

Cahill leaned back onto the hood of his '67 Mustang convertible. He watched Steele as if waiting for a final admonition.

"I thought it was Liana," he said, finally.

Steele stopped his pacing. He turned and looked at Cahill, then took a deep breath.

"We go back on in five minutes," he said. "That's all the time you've got to shake that bitch out of your head."

But as soon as the door swung closed, Cahill knew he wasn't following Steele back on stage. There was no way he was going back inside the Wishing Well.

He slipped behind the wheel of the Mustang, then took off down the alley. He knew what he was doing to the band; he knew what he was doing to Steele. They'd been playing together for the past six years—four on the road backing up a dissolute country crooner named Roan Hyatt, the past two years working the club circuit in L.A.—and now he was running out on him. There was no way to explain it; he wasn't sure he understood it himself. All he knew was that it was over.

He drove across Santa Monica, then headed toward the beach. Venice Boulevard was still thick with traffic. To the west, beyond the crowns of the emaciated palms, hung the dim crescent of a moon. Somewhere in the distance a siren wailed.

He stopped at a liquor store and bought a pint of tequila, then walked back out to his car. All he could think about was the woman at the Wishing Well. He still couldn't believe it wasn't Liana. It wasn't the first time he'd thought he'd seen her; it had happened in nearly every bar, beer hall and roadhouse they'd ever played in.

He twisted the cap off the tequila and took a swallow. He had no idea what to do next. All he knew was that he couldn't go back to his place in Santa Monica. Steele would be coming after him, and that'd be the first place he'd look. He needed a place to crash—just for the night. There was only one place he could think of.

He rocked forward and shoved the pint into the glovebox, then turned the key in the ignition. The engine caught. He revved it up to the red line and then dropped it into gear. The tires howled as he pulled back onto the boulevard and headed for Venice.

He turned into the Canal District, guiding the Mustang over one of the steep, white bridges arching over the water, then turned down a tight, unpaved alley. As the car lurched through the ruts, a pack of dogs ran through the headlights.

He nosed the Mustang into a dilapidated carport, narrowly missing one of the wooden posts that supported the sagging roof, then climbed out of the car and walked up to the gate in a slat fence. He reached over the top and released the latch and let himself into the yard. Through the window in the back of the house, the blue light of a television danced on the wall

He knocked softly on the screen door. He could hear gunplay, slugs ricocheting off rocks. A western was playing on the television.

He slipped inside. Darlene was asleep on the sofa, her head against the padded arm, her legs stretched out across the worn cushions. A bottle of apple wine was on the table in front of the sofa, beside a half-eaten cake still in the pink cardboard box from the bakery. A plastic fork was stabbed into the white frosting.

He leaned down to Darlene and smoothed her thin, brown hair back off her forehead. He had met Darlene and her sister Marilyn shortly after moving to L.A. Late one night, he'd stopped into a self-serve gas station, where she worked as a cashier. She'd just closed the station for the night, but he pleaded that the Mustang was running on fumes. She allowed him to pump a few gallons on the condition that he buy her a cup of coffee. Cahill said he had a better idea. They found an all-night market, bought two thick steaks and a bottle of champagne, then they drove back to his place, where they cooked them on an open grill and drank the champagne as if they both had cause to celebrate.

She was only nineteen. She'd been raised in a town called Shoshone in southern Idaho. When she was fifteen, she and her sister escaped to Los Angeles, ostensibly in search of the father who had run out on them. They never found him, though Darlene, who could scarcely recall what he looked like, held out hope they still would.

She'd thought she would like to become a singer. She had a fine, untrained voice, and Cahill taught her a few chords on the guitar. But her hands were too small to cover the broad neck, and her fingertips too tender to manage the strings; eventually she abandoned both the instrument and the dream and went to work at the gas station, where every night she turned up the radio and sang her way through the shift.

Cahill knew how she'd come to feel about him, and he knew he couldn't let it go on. He'd tried to explain to her about Liana one night as they lay in bed. Darlene said she understood, and he thought she did, but later that night he woke and heard her crying in the bathroom.

She'd married a stock-car driver named Ronnie Hamm while he and Steele were out on the road with Roan Hyatt. One day when the band was passing through town, Cahill called her up, and she invited him over. He met Hamm. He was a hard, wiry man with arms built up with weights and a triangular head driven down into his broad shoulders like the blade of a shovel. Darlene had a crescent-shaped bruise beneath her right eye, but she said she was all right. Cahill didn't press it any further.

Then about a year ago she'd showed up at his house in the middle of the night. He was glad to see her. She confessed that Hamm had fled back to his native Oklahoma or Texas, she wasn't sure which. All he'd left her was a battered Rambler station wagon, but she was glad to be rid of him. They got drunk and then climbed into bed with an enthusiasm they both thought had deserted them.

Cahill sat down beside her on the sofa. He reached for the fork and cut a thick wedge of the cake, then lifted it to his mouth. He washed it down with a slug of the wine as the haze of sleep lifted off her.

"Did you ever think that I might not be alone?" she asked him.

"You look alone to me," he said.

"What if I'd met myself some tall, handsome stranger? Maybe he was going to treat me so good I'd lift right off this sorry planet and float on up to heaven. Did you ever think about that?"

"Do you want me to go?" He set the wine bottle back down on the table. "I'll go."

"No," she said.

She turned toward him and rested her head on his thigh. "You smell like smoke," she said. "I like the way smoke smells on men."

She rolled onto her back and looked up at him. "Men ought to smell like men," she said. "They ought to smell like whatever they're doing, they're doing it hard."

Cahill stared blankly at the television. She pushed up onto her elbows and turned toward him. "What's wrong, cowboy?"

But he couldn't tell her.

She reached out and stroked the side of his face, then patted the sofa. "Lie down," she said.

In the pale glow of the television, she sat astride him and began kneading the base of his neck.

"You'll talk to Steele later," she said with a soft, maternal authority. "You'll sit down over a beer and explain it all to him. He'll understand. He'll have to. But not tonight. You'll stay here tonight."

Cahill filled his lungs with air, then exhaled slowly. "You don't mind?"

She leaned down to him and bit his ear. "When did I get in the habit of saying no to you?"

Then she laughed, freely and easily. She sat

back up and tossed her hair back over her shoulder. "Take off your shirt," she said.

Obediently, he pulled the black, Harley-Davidson T-shirt over his head. He kicked off his hand-tooled boots, then ran both hands back through his hair.

She began massaging his chest. "I was watching a movie on television," she said. "Robert Mitchum was in it. He has such a sad, handsome face. He always makes me cry, just to look at him. He looks like he's suffered so.

"But then I fell asleep, I guess."

She rocked back onto her haunches. "You don't hear a word I'm saying, do you?"

"I'm sorry," he said.

She slid down his legs. He wasn't sure what she was doing until she unclasped his belt.

"No," he said, reaching down to her.

But she had already drawn him out.

"Let me do this for you, cowboy. I don't mind. I want to."

It made him feel worse. When she finished him, she moved up the sofa and lay beside him, between his body and the cushions. She placed her head on his chest.

"I don't mind if you're thinking about her," she said. "I know you can't help it.

"But put your arm around me, will you, cowboy? You can do that for me, can't you?"

* * *

They didn't wake until after noon. As Cahill rolled out of Darlene's bed, he could hear water drilling the walls of the shower. He couldn't recall having risen from the sofa the night before.

He pulled on his jeans and moved into the kitchen, where a life-sized poster of Elvis was tacked up beside the door. In a white sequined suit, the King was snarling into a microphone, a lock of black hair curling down onto his forehead. What looked like a smudge of red lipstick marked his left cheek. As Cahill stepped closer, he saw the lipstick was actually on the poster.

He opened the refrigerator. A cardboard pizza box had been shoved onto the single rack, crowding a handful of withered lemons into the back. A six-pack of diet cola sat in the plastic vegetable tray below. He lifted the lid of the pizza box. White mold covered the remaining slice like a blanket of snow.

Combing out her wet hair, Darlene entered the kitchen as he closed the refrigerator door, her long blue shirt buttoned just once above her navel.

"You can take a shower if you want, only there's no hot water. Marilyn forgot to pay the bill. I don't know what she did with the money, but they came out and turned off the gas."

Cahill sat down at the kitchen table. "Do you need to borrow some money?" he asked. "I could lend you enough to get the gas turned back on."

"Oh no, we'll take care of it," she said.

She leaned over the sink. As she drank from the faucet, the tails of her shirt rode up over her bare buttocks. Wiping her mouth with the back of her hand, she turned back to him. "Would you like a cup of coffee?"

She began rummaging through the cupboards above the sink, rising up onto her toes to search the shelves. "There's a jar of instant here—freeze-dried, I'm sure."

"Actually, I've got to go."

She stopped and turned back to him. "I knew you were going to say that sooner or later.

"Where do you have to go?"

"I just need to get out of here for a few days."

"You can tell me where you're going, can't you?"

Cahill felt the blood rush to his face. He saw how transparent he'd become.

"Look," he said. "Why don't you let me take you out to breakfast?"

She shook her head. "I don't think so. Just call me when you get back in town."

CHAPTER 2

He left Los Angeles late that afternoon. It took all day to drive up Highway 99, the long river of asphalt cleaving through the Central Valley. He stopped only once, near Fresno, where he pulled off the highway to eat at a hamburger stand built in the shape of a huge orange.

By the time he got to Sacramento, darkness had fallen. He caught himself weaving through traffic at nearly eighty miles an hour and forced himself to slow down, but the Mustang seemed to pick up speed of its own volition, as if it could sense its destination.

Finally he could see the Madison Hotel, four stories high and nearly a century old, rising up into the dome of light above Loma Roja. The hotel was the tallest building in town, though its windows and its grand, vaulted entrance had been boarded over for years. He had been in grade school when it was gutted by fire. Standing at the back of the schoolyard, he and the other children had watched it burn. He could still see the flames leaping through the roof, the huge clouds of smoke billowing up into the sky and blocking out the sun.

He drove into town slowly. The streets seemed at once intensely familiar and entirely foreign. Five years had passed since he'd last been home, since he'd come back to help his sister Faith bury their grandfather. Now she was the only family he had left.

She lived on the south side of town, where the small frame houses were neatly arranged in rows, each an image of the next, differing only by color and degree of disrepair. He wondered if she'd be home or if she might still be at Sisters of Mercy, the hospital where she worked as a nurse.

From the end of the block, he could see lights on in her living room. He killed the engine and coasted up to the house, then he stole quietly up to the porch and peered in through the screen door.

She was sitting in an overstuffed chair. A thick paperback lay open in her lap. Her skin was white from working nights. She had high, sharp cheekbones and dark, silken hair. Her eyes were as black as obsidian.

Suddenly she sensed someone watching her. "Who is it?" she shouted, her hand flying up to close the neck of her robe.

She screamed as he pulled open the door. Then she recognized him and bolted out of the chair. She hurled her book at him, furious with him for the fright he had given her.

Cahill laughed as she rushed into his arms.

"You son of a bitch," she cried against his shoulder.

"Oh, you're all right," he said.

Then he noticed David Earle Wagner standing in the doorway behind her, wiping his hands on a dish towel. Faith and Wagner had been living together almost nine years—ever since Wagner returned from San Francisco where he had gone to law school. At least twice Faith had thrown him out, but they'd reconciled each time. That they'd survived at all was a miracle if not necessarily a blessing.

Wagner smiled. Since Cahill had been gone, Wagner's dark hair had taken on streaks of gray, as bright and lustrous as sterling silver. His eyes were pale blue—"liar's eyes," Faith liked to call them.

While still holding Faith, Cahill reached out and shook Wagner's hand. Then Faith pulled out of his arms.

"For the love of Christ, look at you," she said. "There's not enough of your sorry ass to throw a shadow."

"You drive straight through from L.A.?" Wagner asked.

Cahill nodded. Already it seemed an eternity ago.

"Then I'd guess you could use a drink," Wagner said.

"I guess I could."

Faith took Cahill's hand and led him into the kitchen.

"Sit down, sit down," she ordered him.

He sat at the green table pushed against the wall. While Wagner reached into the cupboard and took down a bottle of tequila, Faith grabbed two limes from the refrigerator, then picked the salt shaker off the stovetop and sat down opposite him.

"So tell me what you're doing here," she said, but before he could say a word, she raised the knife to silence him.

"Just don't tell me you woke up this morning and absolutely had to see your kid sister. I'll cut you into bait for lying to me."

"Are you still playing with that Roan Hyatt?" Wagner asked.

Cahill shook his head. "That all fell apart in Reno a couple years ago," he said. "Lately I've been playing with a friend named Paul Steele."

The instant he uttered Steele's name, the bottom seemed to fall out of his stomach. It felt like a lifetime had passed since he'd walked out on the band, but it hadn't even been twenty-four hours. He had no idea what they were doing now. They were supposed to have been playing a dive called the Sky High Club in West L.A.

"I never heard of this Steele," Faith said.

"He was one of the first people I met in L.A. Steele and this drummer named Rudy Dalton were looking for a guitarist, so they put a note up in this guitar shop in Westwood. I saw it and gave them a call. We played together for a couple years."

Faith looked up from the lime she was slicing into wedges. "But you never made any money?"

"That was the only problem."

"Naturally," she said.

"Dalton quit to join another band, and Steele went back to Nashville, where he thought he might be able to get some studio work. I ended up tending bar in a club in Santa Monica where these blonds from UCLA would come down to buy amphetamines from the bikers."

"Now that sounds like a classy establishment," she said.

Cahill shrugged. "It wasn't so bad," he said. "It paid the rent."

He licked the back of his hand, then sprinkled the moist skin with salt.

"Then one night Steele called me from Austin. He'd been playing behind Hyatt for almost six months and their guitarist had just quit, so he told me to fly back to Texas and audition. The next afternoon I sat in with the band for maybe ten minutes, and that dumb bastard Hyatt hired me."

Cahill licked the salt off the back of his hand, tossed back the shot, then bit into a wedge of lime.

"So what happened up in Reno?" Wagner asked.

Cahill tossed the lime peel toward the sink. It skipped across the counter, then bounced onto the floor.

"Hyatt had been married once—he'd married some redhead from Las Vegas, who divorced him as soon as she found out what a whore-chaser he is. Hyatt didn't care. He never paid her any alimony or child support. He had no idea she was living in Sparks, just outside Reno. When she saw a poster that said we were gonna be playing one of the casinos, she talked some judge into issuing a warrant for Hyatt's arrest, and the minute we hit town, they threw him in jail.

"Serves his cheating ass right," Faith observed, but Cahill ignored her.

"So Steele and I went back to L.A. and started another band.

"We've been doing all right," he said. "Only now I'm taking a little time off."

Faith stared across the table at him.

"I still don't get it," she said.

"Get what?"

"What you're doing here, Winn. You don't come home for five years, and then one night you show up without any good reason at all. It doesn't make any sense."

Cahill reached out and took another wedge of lime.

"Unless maybe you came back to see Liana."

They sat around the kitchen table until Faith sucked the last drop of tequila out of the bottle. Then Cahill followed Wagner out of the house.

They walked down the driveway, past the black-and-white Dodge Polaris that Wagner had purchased from the highway patrol at a state auction years ago and then restored to the agency's high performance specifications. The driveway was scored with skid marks.

"So how's business?" Cahill asked.

"Crime is up. Business is good, Winn. I even have a secretary now. She comes in three days a week, types a few briefs, sorts the mail. On her good days, she makes a few threatening telephone calls.

"Naturally Faith thinks I'm screwing her."

"You two seem to be getting along as well as ever."

Wagner waved his hand through the air, dismissing the acrimony that hung between the two of them. "She's just got a bug up her ass about the other night," Wagner said.

He pointed at the stub of a wooden mailbox post protruding from the bare ground beside the driveway, then smiled. "I was out celebrating another brilliant legal victory over the district attorney."

Cahill laughed as he walked out to the Mustang. Wagner had a reputation as an attorney with an attitude. He'd take any client that could manage the three flights of stairs to his office in the Woodrow Building downtown. He especially enjoyed those hapless criminal cases referred to him by the court when the public defender's office was too busy or hopelessly compromised. To bill his time to the county for publicly humiliating Stanton Douglas, the bald, beet-faced district attorney, was an opportunity he lived to seize.

Cahill slid behind the wheel of his car.

"Are you gonna make it out to Hudson Grove tomorrow?" Wagner asked.

Cahill didn't know what he meant.

"To the picnic," Wagner said.

Then Cahill allowed himself a laugh. He hadn't even realized tomorrow was the Fourth of July.

"You know she'll be there," Wagner said.

He drove back across town to the old man's house. It looked exactly the same as it had five years ago. The dark green shutters were pinned back against the white clapboard walls. The plank steps leading up to the porch listed severely to the left. The spine of the shingled roof swayed beneath the weight of the sky. All that was missing was Francis Robert in his chair on the porch, sipping whiskey from a mason jar and smoking his hand-rolled cigarettes down to the tips of his yellowed fingers.

He was a small man, no more than five and a half feet tall, with bandy legs and a thick moustache that flowed down over his mouth. He'd been born in Grand Junction, Colorado, but he left there when he was fifteen years old to work the rodeo circuit. He rode broncs and bulls and even made a little money tying calves, but eventually the rodeo took its toll on him. In Calgary a calf kicked him in the face, fracturing his cheek and almost costing him an eye. Two years later he was thrown by a bull in Red Bluff, and his right leg jackknifed like a diesel rig in the rain.

After recuperating all winter in Red Bluff, he drifted down the valley that spring to Loma Roja, where he went to work for the Drummond ranch, running cattle up into summer pasture in the Sierras. He worked for Rawley Drummond for forty-three years before arthritis locked up his bad leg. He'd been retired to the front porch for almost ten years when he took in Faith and Winn after their mother died.

Cahill climbed out of the Mustang, then reached into the back seat and lifted out his duffel bag and guitar. As he carried them up to the house, he realized he could scarcely recall what their real father looked like. Except for the small framed photograph their mother used to keep by the side of her bed, he'd never even seen the man their mother dropped out of high school to marry.

His name was Douglas Cooper, which now seemed as remote and unfamiliar as his face. The photograph had been taken at the naval station in San Diego. Smartly dressed in his seaman's whites, he was standing in front of the solemn gray hull of an aircraft carrier, offering an exaggerated salute to the camera. Their mother had taken the photograph. She'd gone down to spend a week of shore leave with him, and they'd driven out into the desert and holed up in a highway motel for seven days.

Then he shipped back out to sea. Three months later, they were notified that he had died in Okinawa. The official word from the navy was that he had succumbed to an undetermined disease, but later they received a letter from another seaman who informed them that he'd died from bad liquor smuggled aboard the ship.

Their mother never recovered from his death. That winter she came down with valley fever. For a week she writhed in bed, drenched with sweat and tortured by hallucinations, and then she was gone. The doctor said it was a shame she hadn't put up more of a fight.

For them her death left only Francis Robert, who took them in without complaint, asking only that they take his last name.

When Cahill had left for Los Angeles, the old man was still as cantankerous as he'd ever been, but Cahill could see his health was beginning to fail. He was in Great Falls, Montana, playing behind Hyatt, when he got a telegram from Faith that said Francis Robert had passed away. Cahill caught a plane back to San Francisco and then over to Sacramento, where Wagner met him at the airport and then drove him up to Loma Roja. The next day they laid him to rest in the cemetery north of town.

Cahill propped the screen door open with his knee, then unlocked the front door and stepped inside. The temperature had to have risen above a hundred degrees that afternoon. The house was hot, the air stale and baked. He turned on a light and walked over to the swamp cooler in the window. He plugged the cooler in and turned it on. As it rumbled to life, he pulled his T-shirt over his head and then leaned against the wall, letting the cool air blow against his bare chest.

Liana had come to the funeral. That was the last time he'd seen her. She was standing beneath one of the eucalyptus trees, the wind lifting her long blond hair off the shoulders of her black dress, her hand slipped through the arm of Michael Harris. Afterward she and Michael dropped by the gathering at the house. Cahill was smoking a cigarette in the backyard when she stepped out onto the back porch and then started down to him.

She smiled cautiously as she stood in front of him. "I'm sorry about Francis Robert," she said.

Cahill nodded, but he had no idea what to say to her. It had been three years since he'd left for Los Angeles.

"How long are you going to be home?" she asked him.

"I'm not sure," he said.

"Will you come out and see me before you go?"

Suddenly he felt like everyone there was watching them. He looked up at the house. Faith and Michael were standing on the porch. They turned and pushed back inside when they saw he'd noticed them.

She had seen them too. "Come out tomorrow," she said.

"I don't know, Liana."

"Promise me," she said, urgency rising in her voice.

He laughed. "I promise," he said, and then he watched her run back into the house.

But of course he hadn't gone out to see her. Michael was still alive.

Instead he left the next morning; and now, as he dropped down onto the sofa and pulled off his boots, he wondered if she'd truly expected him to drive out to the Harris ranch, or if she'd known all along, even as she pressed for his promise, that he wouldn't.

CHAPTER 3

NOT QUITE TEN miles west of town, Hudson Grove was a stand of valley oaks on the east bank of the Sacramento River. With red, white and blue bunting looped across the stage, a wooden bandstand stood in the heart of the grove, surrounded by tables covered with red and white cloth. Smoke lifted from the fire pits and drifted through the trees. Children chased each other down the grassy slope to the edge of the river, where a group of men and boys were playing softball in a clearing transformed into a makeshift diamond.

Faith was sitting alone at one of the tables, idly watching the softball game. Wagner stood out in left field, his glove on his hip and a can of beer in his other hand.

Cahill walked down to her. When she heard him approaching, she turned around.

"I knew you'd show up," she said as Cahill lifted the lid off a red metal cooler and dug a can of beer from the bed of ice. "I told Liana you'd be here."

She paused, waiting for a response. When none came, she said, "I called and told her you were home for a few days."

Cahill opened the can, then took a drink. "How is she?"

"She said she wants to see you."

"Is that right," he said.

Faith picked up a piece of carrot, then snapped it off in her teeth. "It's been a long time, Winn. She's gone through a lot since you've been gone. She's changed. We've all changed."

Cahill took another swallow of beer. "Sure we have," he said.

"What do you want from her?"

He laughed. The question was ridiculous, absurd. "Maybe I just want to put an end to it," he said.

"That's what I was afraid of," Faith said.

He walked down the bank to the river, the last of the sunlight glinting on the rippled surface. A great blue heron spread its wings and waved across the water. He watched it land on a raft of hyacinth at the mouth of Jessel Slough, then took another sip of beer.

For three years he and Liana had lived in an old farmhouse out on Kingdom Road. Liana had found the house. It was a good twenty miles south of town, near the stables where she boarded the old mare named Highway she'd had since she was a girl. The house had been empty for almost a year, but they hacked down the star thistle and Johnson grass and planted flowers in the raised brick beds. With a fresh coat of paint, it suited them fine.

He'd been playing in a band called the Wheels, but the money was thin and the music ragged, so he quit and hired on at the Whitney ranch. It was hard, back-breaking work, especially during harvest when they worked fourteen-hour days every day for six or eight straight weeks, but he didn't mind. Liana worked in the pharmacy in town. When they both got home in the evening, they'd walk out to the canal that ran behind the house and spread out a blanket on the side of the levee. As the moon rose above the Sierra, they'd drink a bottle of wine and smoke a joint, then plot out their dreams like they were charting constellations in a distant galaxy.

Liana wanted to go to Mexico. It took them a year to save the money. In January, they drove the Mustang down to Baja, all the way to Cabo San Lucas. They were on their way home, staying at the old beach hotel in Rosarito, when she told him she was pregnant. She'd thought so before they left; now she knew for sure. She'd been afraid to say anything, afraid he wouldn't want the child. She couldn't believe he wanted it as much as she did.

They returned to Loma Roja the next day. The pregnancy bloomed on her face. In the mornings he'd draw down the sheet and study her flat stomach for any sign of a bulge; he'd press his ear to her taut skin, listening for that first elusive beat of a new heart. There was nothing he could do but comfort her as she braved the morning sickness. Later, when she began to tire easily, he'd help her to bed, and he'd run a brush through her hair until she fell asleep.

Then one night he woke to her throttled sobbing. He found her doubled over on the bathroom floor and raced her in to Sisters of Mercy, but he knew, even before they wheeled her into the emergency room, that she'd miscarried.

When he brought her home, she wouldn't talk to him. The silence lasted for days that turned into weeks. She quit her job. With her head propped up on the arm of the couch, she watched television all day and night, numbing her loss with red wine. He knew she was in pain, but he couldn't reach her.

Finally she moved out. He came home from the Whitney ranch one night to find her carrying her clothes to her car. All she could say was that she had to leave. He knew enough to let her go.

He stayed in the house for almost a year after she left, clinging to the hope that somehow they might find their way back to each other. But there was no single incident for which to plead for understanding, no indiscretion for which to beg forgiveness. Liana would see him only rarely. Desperate, he told her one night that he was thinking about moving to Los Angeles.

"I want to start playing in a band again," he said.

Her eyes lit up. "Oh, you should!" she exclaimed. "I can't stand to see you wasting yourself out at the Whitney ranch. You're too good for that, Winn. You've got so much talent. You don't know how sad it made me when you quit playing with the Wheels."

"I hired on at the Whitney ranch for you," he said. "We needed the money."

But she had no intention of arguing with him. She reached across the table and took his hand. "I'm so happy for you, Winn. Honest to God I am. When are you leaving?"

Suddenly he realized that he hadn't given a moment's thought to Los Angeles. It had all been a hollow threat. All he wanted was for her to urge him to stay. But as he looked across the booth at her, he realized he was committed.

"Tomorrow," he'd said, and the next morning he'd headed south, hating her for not stopping him.

He spotted her as she was walking through the trees, down the muddy bank to the beach to watch the fireworks. She stopped and looked back up the bank. The crowd streamed past her. She didn't move, like a deer frozen in a beam of light.

From behind, Wagner grabbed him by the arm.

"Let's go," he said.

Cahill turned around to him.

"The fireworks are about to start. Faith's waiting," Wagner said. "She's got a place staked out just above the beach."

Then Wagner smiled, as if to laugh at him, and Cahill knew he'd seen her too.

In rapid succession, three shells were fired from the opposite bank of the river. The crowd along the bank roared as the fireballs exploded overhead, their searing, phosphorescent trails streaking across the sky. On the bandstand, the band performed patriotic marches and anthems. Children waved sparklers through the smoky air.

Faith leaned back on the blanket she had spread out on the grass. She rested her head on Wagner's crossed legs and handed Cahill a joint. He pinched it in his fingertips, then filled his lungs with the harsh smoke and lay back on the grass. He wondered what Liana had been looking for as she gazed back up the bank.

When the band took up the national anthem, they knew the fireworks were over.

"It gets shorter every year," Faith complained as she gathered up the blanket and started back up into the grove of oaks.

"Indisputable evidence that Western civilization continues its inglorious decline," Wagner observed.

"Are you staying for the dance?" Cahill asked.

"You bet your ass he is," Faith said.

A group of bluegrass musicians—a stocky, bearded guitarist, a banjo player in a dark blue beret, a stand-up bassist and a tall, thin, reedy-voiced fiddler Cahill recognized as Leo Hill— had claimed the bandstand from the marching band. Already a dozen couples were dancing on the bare, compacted soil in front of the stage.

Cahill stood back behind the rows of wooden chairs that ringed the dancing area and watched Faith and Wagner move into the crowd. It didn't take them ten bars to look as if they were dancing to two entirely different songs. Faith followed the jig played by Hill; Wagner preferred a slow, lumbering beat that only he could hear. It didn't seem to bother either of them.

Suddenly he felt someone behind him.

"What's a girl have to do to get you to ask her to dance?"

Cahill placed his hand on the small of her back. Liana gathered herself up to him. She was inordinately warm, her skin almost hot to the touch.

When the fiddle finally trailed away, she pulled back and looked up at him, her eyes the color of blued steel.

"Tell me how you've been," she said. "You look good."

"It's the exemplary lifestyle I lead."

Her mouth formed an effortless smile. "Like a holy man, I'm sure. Faith told me you'd come home," she said.

"She's not one to keep a secret."

Liana laughed. "No, she's not."

The music resumed. She extended her hand. "One more?"

He didn't resist her.

As they moved back into the crowd, he caught her glancing past him, over his shoulder. He turned but couldn't tell what she saw.

"I'm sorry," she said suddenly. "I've got to go."

"What's wrong?"

He reached out to her, but she eluded him, then cut across the crowded dance area. He started after her, brushing past an elderly couple, then nearly colliding with a middle-aged woman in a bright blue dress.

Then he saw her at the edge of the dancing area, standing beside Tommy Gillespie, steadying herself as she bent down and slipped into her sandals.

Tommy's hair was combed back, as black as the T-shirt tucked into his pleated white trousers. The sleeves of his summer sports coat were bunched up at the elbows. When he spotted Cahill he grinned broadly, then pulled away from Liana and walked over to him.

"Well, isn't this a pleasant surprise?"

"Hello, Tommy."

"You're back in town, Winn. What a great honor for us."

Cahill didn't say anything.

"I hope you're enjoying the picnic," he said. He waved his hand through the air, gesturing toward the stars. "Did you like the fireworks?"

Liana approached Tommy from behind and touched his arm. "Let's go, Tommy," she said.

"Did you enjoy dancing with Liana?"

Cahill looked over to Liana. Her eyes begged him to back away.

"I think we should leave," she said.

"You were dancing together, weren't you?" Tommy pressed. "For old times' sake?"

Cahill took a deep breath. "I think she wants to leave," he said.

Tommy turned to her. "Is that so?"

She nodded.

"Why didn't you say something?"

"Please, Tommy," she said.

He turned back to Cahill. "I wish we could talk more, Winn, but Liana wants me to take her home. What Liana wants, Liana gets—you remember that, don't you?"

Then Tommy laughed at him. He took Liana by the arm and led her away. All Cahill could do was watch them disappear into the trees.

"What the hell was that all about?" Wagner asked, stepping up beside him.

Only then did Cahill realize that he was

standing alone in the middle of the dancing area, that all the other dancers had moved away from him. He could feel their eyes on him, as hot as fire.

"Take a fucking guess," he said.

CHAPTER 4

HE STOMPED DOWN hard on the gas. The Mustang's tires bit into the loose gravel, spraying pieces of rock behind. The convertible lunged forward, dragging the transmission through the ruts at the mouth of the parking lot. He sped down Pacheco Road, pounding the steering wheel with the heel of his hand, furious that he'd allowed Tommy Gillespie to humiliate him.

As he left Hudson Grove behind and headed back to town, he reached across the dashboard and released the glovebox door, then fumbled through the maps and registration papers until he located the pint of tequila. He took a long pull. As the road straightened out, he wedged the bottle between his thighs. He knew Liana didn't care about Tommy. No one could tell him she did.

He saw the train in the corner of his eye. No more than half a mile away, it was headed south on tracks built up like a levee bank, its headlamp slashing through the night. Dead ahead, the two pulsing red lights at the crossing warned of the train's approach. He could hear the clanging bell, the steel wheels clattering on the rails. He had no intention of waiting for the train to pass and pressed down on the accelerator. He knew he could beat it.

As the Mustang raced toward the crossing, he could feel the front wheels kicking up on the pocked, two-lane road; he gripped the steering wheel hard to keep the car from veering off into the ditch along the shoulder. In the air rushing over the windshield, he felt giddy, euphoric. At seventy-five miles an hour, the Mustang would sail into flight when it swept up over the elevated tracks. He had no idea what might be on the opposite side; he didn't care.

The train was bearing down on the crossing. Its whistle sounded, louder than he'd expected—a long, ominous moan followed by another. Suddenly he realized it was going to be closer than he'd thought.

His stomach turned sickly sweet. A voice in the back of his head shouted for him to back off. He held his breath, then stomped down hard on the accelerator, flattening the pedal to the floorboards.

Then he saw the crossing arm descending across the road. He realized he wasn't going to make it. He hit the brakes so hard he nearly lifted from the seat. The tires locked up, howling as the Mustang slid sideways down the road, but it was too late. He couldn't stop in time.

The Mustang crashed broadside through the wooden crossing arm, then rocked up onto its left side. Instinctively he raised both arms to protect his face. For an instant, he thought the Mustang would roll completely over.

Instead it dropped back down, righting itself, and then the train was roaring past, the blast of its whistle so loud he winced, the roadbed shaking beneath its rolling weight. Then he heard laughter. It took him a minute to recognize it as his own.

He drove into town to a bar called the Blue Orchid. The Blue Orchid had been the old man's bar of choice. Francis Robert's picture, along with those of several dozen others who had sought their absolution there, hung on the wall above the jukebox. The grainy black-and-white photographs had been taken during the Great Depression. All the men had been in their twenties and thirties when the portraits had been shot. Like soldiers photographed in combat, they looked distantly related, if not by blood then at least by circumstance. Small gold stars, pasted into the lower right-hand corners of the frames by the bartender, identified those who had passed away.

The bartender's name was Buckley. Buckley's father had taken the photographs on the wall, and he remembered Cahill as Francis Robert's boy, even if that wasn't strictly true.

"Give me a shot of tequila and a glass of draft back," Cahill said.

Buckley lifted the bottle of tequila from the rack behind the bar. "Why aren't you out at Hudson Grove?" he asked.

"I was out there," Cahill said.

Buckley brought the shot of tequila over. Cahill threw it back, then reached for the glass of beer. His heart was still pounding in his chest.

"See anyone you know?"

Cahill laughed acidly. "Does Tommy Gillespie count?"

Buckley smiled, then leaned back and crossed his arms and watched Cahill take a long drink of beer.

"You know his old man bought the James ranch a couple years ago—twelve thousand acres of dry pasture up in the foothills."

"What the hell does Calvin Gillespie know about running cattle?" Cahill asked.

Buckley shrugged. "Calvin doesn't care about cattle. He just wanted to build himself a house up there on the bluff above Holmes Creek. It's a goddamn mansion, took two years to finish—it's even got a marble fountain. At night, all lit up with floodlights, you can see the damn thing twenty miles away."

Buckley lit a cigarette, then laid it in a blue

glass ashtray. "Calvin's even got himself a new wife these days," he said.

"How many does that make?"

"That's number five—one for each of his Chevy dealerships. This one's named Miranda. She was in one of his television commercials. She's only a couple years older than Tommy. She looks like his sister. Of course, she and Tommy don't get along so good, I hear."

Cahill drained the glass of beer, then pushed it out for Buckley to fill again. "Nobody gets along with Tommy," he said. "Not for long, anyway. All he cares about is that bored-out Camaro."

Buckley laughed. "Tommy hasn't been driving that Camaro for a couple years now. He was racing some Pontiac out on the Midway and blew a tire and spun off into an orchard. He totalled the Camaro."

"Nothing happened to him?"

"He broke his collarbone."

"That's it?"

Buckley filled Cahill's glass, then slid it back to him. "I guess he's just lucky, Winn."

Cahill took a sip of the beer. "So what did the old man buy him after that?"

"A black 'forty-eight Chevy pickup. I used to see him every Friday night, cruising through town with his tape deck blaring and his latest girlfriend propped up beside him like a carnival doll. I haven't seen much of him lately, though."

Buckley reached for his cigarette and took a drag, sucking the thick smoke in through his nose.

"You and Tommy have some trouble tonight?"

Cahill sipped at his beer. "Tommy thinks anything he wants is his."

"You got something he wants?"

"I did once," Cahill said.

"I see," Buckley said. He dropped a white towel on the bar and gave it a cursory wipe, then poured Cahill another shot of tequila, along with one for himself.

"I hear Tommy's been seeing Liana Harris," Buckley said.

Cahill threw his shot back, then shoved the shotglass out for Buckley to fill it again.

"Is that a fact," he said.

"Last call," Buckley said.

"Then give me two more," Cahill said.

"One of them's for me," said a woman sitting two stools to Cahill's right.

Cahill turned toward her. The three ranchers who had been playing cards at the table near the jukebox had left. She was the only other patron in the Blue Orchid.

She had on billowly white pants and a blue blouse cut low to reveal a deep, cultivated tan. She offered Cahill a slanted smile.

When he didn't say anything, she slipped off her stool and made her way down to him. As

Buckley brought over the two glasses of draft, she hiked a leg up onto the railing at the foot of the bar. Cahill watched her raise the glass to her mouth. She closed her eyes as she drank.

"Let me give you a piece of advice," she said, pointing a finger at Cahill's chest, then stabbing him with the long, sharp nail.

"Don't never marry yourself an Indian. They're amorous as all get out, but they've got unnatural desires."

She gripped the padded edge of the bar with both hands. "I love that goddamn Maidu. God knows I love him. But I don't need to tell you what he wants from me. I think you can imagine. Do you think I'd ever give that son of a bitch what he wants?"

She shook her head slowly, emphatically, her mouth curled up in disgust. "You've got to draw the line. You've got to draw the line somewhere."

She stopped for a moment. She took a deep breath. "I've never cheated on that man," she declared proudly. "That's not the way I am."

"Good for you," Cahill said.

"That's not what you're thinking, though, is it?" She stared directly at his mouth. "You were thinking there's a first time for everything, weren't you?" She smiled brightly, confidently.

"Not exactly."

"Like hell you weren't," she snapped. She raised her hand as if to slap him across the face.

He didn't flinch, knowing he could catch her wrist before she could strike him.

Slowly a smile broke over her face. "You don't look like a man who allows himself to be hit," she said as she lowered her hand.

Cahill shrugged. "I didn't think you'd do it," he said.

"You're pretty smart, aren't you?" She smiled, then sniffled as if about to sneeze, then rubbed the tip of her nose on the palm of her hand.

Then a look of puzzlement spread over her face. "I don't even know your name."

"Winn."

"Like winners and losers."

"More like winners, actually."

She smiled, then turned to regard herself in the mirror on the wall behind the bar, carefully selecting her reflection from amid the rows of bottles. She patted her frosted hair into place, tilting her head as if to examine herself from another angle.

"I'm Valentina," she said. "As in Valentine's Day."

"That's a lovely name," Cahill said.

She smiled at him. "What do you say we go get ourselves a motel room, Mr. Winner?"

She didn't wait for an answer. She whirled around to the bartender.

"And if that goddamn Indian calls, you tell him me and the winner here took off to have ourselves a fine old time."

Cahill drained his glass and stood up. He looked at Buckley.

"What the hell," he said.

They pushed out of the Blue Orchid. As they made their way down the sidewalk, Cahill took Valentina by the arm, just above the elbow. His thumb and forefinger met at the bone. He wasn't particularly amused to learn she had no intention of going to a motel, but he wasn't inclined to press the issue. On the road with Hyatt and then back in L.A., he'd spent enough nights with women like her to know how bad his life would taste in the morning.

As she stood beside her Lincoln Continental, she told him she had only been putting the bartender on.

"It's all a mind game," she said, lifting up her car keys and rattling them in his face. "Sometimes I like to play with people's minds a little. Life's a mind game, if you want my opinion."

A tiny black coiffeured poodle was standing on the front seat, its bobbed tail quivering, its bark frenzied and sharp. She swept the poodle up off the seat as she slipped behind the wheel, then pressed it to her face and kissed it on the nose.

"Her name is Sassy," Valentina said as she positioned the poodle in her lap. "She's very protective. She just might give you a nip, just to show you who's boss."

She rolled up the window and started the engine, and then she waved at him and the Continental pulled away. He watched her drive down the block until she disappeared around the corner.

He walked back up the street to the Mustang, then drove back to the old man's house in defeat.

He parked in the driveway and climbed out of the car. An envelope was pinned to the screen door. He crossed the yard and stepped up onto the porch.

He recognized Liana's smooth handwriting the instant he tore the envelope open.

CHAPTER 5

THE HARRIS RANCH was seven miles southwest of Loma Roja. As Cahill raced out the Midway he could see the long row of palms that branched off the road and led into the ranch, tracking across the flooded fields like islands in an archipelago, their towering crowns swaying beneath the hard white moon.

He'd never known Michael Harris—only who he was. His mother was Lillian Harris, whose father had been one of the first ranchers to settle the valley. Michael was Lillian Harris's only son. He was tall and lean, a fluid, natural athlete who starred in football in high school. They said he might even have had a shot to play professionally, but he tore up a knee in college and was never even drafted. Cahill had nothing against him. Now that he was dead, what did it matter that he'd married Liana?

He turned in through the gate to the ranch, then followed the dirt road that ran along the base of the palms to the sprawling Spanish-style house rising quietly from behind a high white wall. He pulled up in front of the court-yard.

The condition of the house surprised him. Beneath its red tile roof, broad sheets of paint were peeling off the troweled plaster walls. Rust bled down from the corners of the iron-framed windows. The gardens that surrounded the courtyard had long since gone to jungle.

He had no idea what Liana wanted. The note said only to come see her out at the ranch. Even after what had happened at Hudson Grove, she knew he'd come.

He walked up to the house and knocked on the heavy wooden door. No one answered, so he reached down and tried the latch. The door swung open easily on its forged iron hinges.

He leaned inside. "Liana?" he called into the house, but she didn't answer.

He stepped inside. As tentatively as a thief, he made his way through the house. Through the arched entrance to the living room, several rattan chairs gathered before the stone hearth of the fireplace. On a heavy chain, a huge iron chandelier hung from the rough-hewn beams of the ceiling. A silver vase of roses stood on a writing table at the foot of the stairs. Their sweet fragrance filled the foyer.

Suddenly he began to worry about her.

"Liana?" he called out again, louder than before.

But then he saw her. Through the glass-panel doors that opened onto the terraced gardens, she was hurrying toward the house, her long white dress sailing out behind her.

"You came," she said, and then she laughed at the sight of him as if delighted with herself. She clasped her hands beneath her chin. "You found my note."

She moved toward him and slipped her arms around his waist. They embraced for only a moment before he pulled away, abruptly remembering his humiliation at the dance.

"Let me get you a beer," she said.

As she disappeared down the dark hall leading to the kitchen, Cahill walked outside. The patio was illuminated by the ominous blue glow of the pool. Brass lanterns burned in the gardens across the pool, the flames dancing on the surface of the water. The water lapped at the mosaic tile, warping the long diamonds of light created by the underwater lamp.

He turned as Liana emerged from the house, a snifter of brandy in one hand, a bottle of beer in the other.

"Where's Tommy?" he asked her.

Her face tensed. She handed him the beer. "You don't waste any time, do you?"

"It's a fair question."

"I'm sorry," she said. "That was stupid, wasn't it? I never should have asked you to dance."

Cahill sipped at the beer. "I didn't know you were seeing him," he said.

Liana sat down in one of the lounge chairs

arranged around the pool. She covered her knees with the dress.

"It's not like you think," she said. "We're not a couple."

Cahill looked up at the long sweeping limbs of the Monterey pines, sighing in the breeze.

She brushed her hair back over her shoulder. "Don't be so angry with me," she said. "I made Tommy bring me home, then I drove into town looking for you. You can't fault me for that."

"What did you say to him?"

"Tonight?"

"To lose him."

She took a sip of brandy. "I told him I wasn't feeling well."

He took another sip of beer. Even if he didn't understand what she saw in Gillespie, he took no little satisfaction in knowing she'd deceived him on his behalf.

"You look fine to me," he said.

"I'm experiencing a dramatic recovery."

She must have seen the hunger in his eyes. She led him upstairs. At the foot of the bed she lifted her dress over her head and shook out her hair, then she drew him down to her.

It seemed so smooth, so effortless. Suddenly he couldn't trust it. She clutched wildly at him as he pulled away from her. Her mouth opened; she sucked at the vaporous air. He struggled up onto his knees, then dragged her across the mattress and lifted her onto him. Tears slid down the sides of her face. A moan rose low in her throat. She shuddered hard, her arms around his neck, then she collapsed back onto the bed.

On his hands and knees, he stretched out above her, sweat running down his face, dripping onto her. She raised up and took his bottom lip in her teeth and pulled him down to her. She reached up and ran her fingertips down his spine, then down his buttocks and the backs of his thighs.

He laid down beside her. She rolled toward him and rested her head on his chest as if listening to his heart. Across the room, shadows flickered on the wall, thrown by the candle burning down into itself on the nightstand beside the bed. He ran his hand through her hair and let it curl around his fingers.

But then he couldn't lie there any longer.

"What are you doing?" she asked as he slipped out from beneath her.

"I can't breathe," he said.

He picked his jeans off the bench in front of the vanity, then moved out onto the balcony, where the breeze moving down the valley cooled him off.

After a minute, he walked back into the bedroom and sat on the bench in front of the vanity.

"Why did you want me to come out here tonight?"

"I wanted to see you. I was afraid you'd leave and I'd never see you—like the last time you were here. You promised you'd come out. I waited all day for you. Finally I called Faith, and she told me you'd left to go back to Montana or wherever it was."

"You like to forget the fact that you were married," he said. "You married Michael as soon as I was gone. I wasn't in L.A. a month when you married him."

'You knew I was seeing him," she said softly.

"Suddenly it all made sense why you wanted me to go to L.A. so bad."

"That's not true," she said, pushing up on the mattress. "You wanted to play in a band again. You couldn't do that here. Moving to Los Angeles was best for you. That's all I wanted."

"I'd say it worked out well for you, too."

She dropped back onto the bed and gazed up at the ceiling. "It didn't work out so well," she said.

"When Lillian Harris died, you ended up with one of the finest ranches in the valley." He laughed. "I'd say you could have done worse—like if you'd stayed with me."

"Lillian hated me. I was never good enough for her Michael. The old woman went crazy when he told her we were getting married. She refused to hear of it. We held the ceremony here, and she didn't come out of her room the whole day. She just sat up here with the curtains pulled and drank a bottle of gin.

"We lived in town so she could stay here at the ranch, but she was so mean to the nurses that they'd quit after a couple of days or a week. She wouldn't let me help her, of course. Finally, because of her hip, she couldn't make it up the stairs anymore, so we had to move her into town.

"It was nice, Winn. It really was. She had her own room with a color television. But she hated it, of course, and she blamed me for it. I took her flowers from the gardens, I'd take her peaches and apricots and apples from the trees behind the corral, but she wouldn't even talk to me.

"She complained to Michael day and night. It was hard on him—I know it was. He started in drinking, only it made him mean. Twice he got himself arrested in town—once for kicking in a storefront window, another time for fighting I don't even know what about. I'd have to go down to the jail to get him, and naturally the sheriff and all the deputies would look at me like it was my fault.

"Then one afternoon I was out at the corral when I heard a shot. At first I thought maybe someone was poaching a pheasant out at the back of the ranch—it sounded distant like that, muffled. Then I remembered Michael was in the basement, loading shells, and suddenly I knew what had happened. I ran back to the house and then down the stairs. God, it was awful."

Cahill took a swallow of beer, then wiped his mouth on the back of his arm. He let a moment pass.

"Did they ever determine what happened?"

"They never found any note, if that's what you mean." Then she laughed angrily. "But no one ever believed it was an accident, either."

She rubbed her eyes with the heels of her hands. "I have Melissa Macklin to thank for that."

"Who's she?"

"Melissa? She lived out on the river, in one of those trailers at Eden's Landing. Michael met her in the bar there. I knew about her the whole time. I knew he was sleeping with her. I told him I knew. He never even tried to lie his way out of it.

"The day after Michael died, Melissa told Lillian that Michael wanted to divorce me. That's all Lillian needed to hear. She told anyone who'd listen that I'd killed Michael because I was afraid he was gonna leave me for her. After that, no one believed me, not even after Dan Cassidy, my foreman, told the sheriff that he'd heard the shot too and then saw me running toward the house.

"Even that didn't stop the old woman. She claimed Cassidy was lying. She claimed he was trying to protect me because we were having an affair behind Michael's back.

"Can you believe that? It ruined Cassidy. When his wife read that in the newspaper, she just packed up and took off back to Missouri.

"It was horrible," she said. "Everyday I'd wake up and there'd be dead cats hung from the arch at the gate. I don't know who did it. I don't care. I don't want to know. They'd just hang there until Cassidy cut them down.

"Anytime I went into town people would stare at me. I felt like Faith and David Earle were my only friends. I felt like a prisoner out here."

As Cahill took another swallow of beer, she beckoned him over to the bed.

"Come here, baby," she said.

He stood up and walked over. He stretched out beside her.

"I'm so glad you're home—even if it's only for a few days."

He slid down her chest. He teased a broad dark nipple with the tip of his tongue until it hardened, then he bit her gently. A long sigh issued from her mouth through lips drawn back as if wincing in pain.

She reached down to him. Her hands slid along the sides of his face. Her fingers traced the rim of his jaw as he dragged his tongue between her breasts.

Suddenly the flare of a match lit the room. Liana screamed. Cahill leapt up off the bed.

Tommy was standing in the doorway.

* * *

He raised the match to the tip of his cigarette, then waved it out and tilted his head to exhale toward the ceiling. "I'm not breaking anything up, am I?"

"Get out of here!" Liana screamed at him.

Tommy turned to Cahill and leveled a cold smile. "Liana's not feeling well tonight. Did she tell you that, Winn? That's what she told me. She said she didn't want me to catch anything."

He smiled again. "Wasn't that thoughtful of the little bitch?"

Cahill took a step toward him. "Get out of here, Tommy."

"Or what, Winn? What are you going to do?"

Cahill stared at Tommy, waiting, saying nothing. He didn't know what to do. He felt guilty as an accomplice to Liana's deceit, but he was also angry, not simply that he had been caught with her but that Tommy believed he possessed some claim to her.

Tommy laughed, then inhaled deeply on his cigarette. "You know, Winn, I can't say I was surprised to see your Mustang parked out front."

"She wants you to leave, Tommy. You want to talk, we can talk tomorrow."

"Talk?" he snapped, his voice abruptly growing hard. "Talk about what?"

"Please, Tommy," Liana implored him. "Please."

Tommy glared at her. "She tells me she's

sick, so I come out to look in on her, and she's in bed with you.''

''You're a son of a bitch!'' she hissed.

Tommy laughed, then flicked his cigarette through the glass doors opening onto the balcony. ''So what's there to talk about?''

''Just take off, Tommy, before this gets any worse.''

Tommy spun around to him. ''How's it gonna get any worse?''

Before Cahill could say anything, Liana flew at Tommy. He was waiting for her; he slapped her across the face with the back of his hand. When she came at him again, he threw her to the floor.

''That's enough!'' Cahill shouted.

He lunged for Tommy's arm, but Tommy jerked free and then shoved Cahill backward, pounding Cahill's shoulders with the heels of his hands.

''Let it go, Tommy!''

He heard the blade click into position. He didn't understand what the sound meant until the knife flashed in front of him.

''Come on, Winn,'' Tommy urged him. ''Show me what you've got.''

Sweat flooded down Cahill's brow, streaming into his eyes. ''Don't do this, Tommy. Just turn and go. You can still walk out of here.''

But Tommy wasn't listening as he advanced on him. He slashed at him. Cahill leaped back out of the way as the blade sliced through the air.

"What the fuck are you doing?" Cahill shouted. He glanced past him, across the room to the door, but there was no way to reach it. He could feel Tommy working him into the corner of the room, like a prizefighter controlling the ring.

"Tommy!" screamed Liana.

A baleful smile crossed Tommy's face. Even in the dim light, his eyes were hard and small as rivets. "Watch me," he said, and then he slashed at Cahill again.

Cahill jumped back out of the way until his back pressed up against the cool plaster wall. Tommy raised the knife and held it up between them as if he meant for Cahill to contemplate what it was about to do to him. There was nowhere left for Cahill to go.

Then suddenly the room was filled with light, the flash of the muzzle at Tommy's back. Cahill spun away and then doubled over, recoiling from the deafening concussion.

"No!" he heard himself scream.

CHAPTER 6

A MOMENT PASSED—an eternity—before the shot's report faded out of the room. Cahill had no idea how long he'd been standing there before he knelt down beside Tommy. He pressed a finger to the veins in Tommy's neck, but already his pulse had deserted him.

As he rose to his feet, his skin crawled on him.

He spun around to Liana. She dropped the pistol onto the bed, then shrank back against the wall.

"What was I supposed to do?" she cried. "He would have killed you!"

"Tommy knew what you were doing. He knew you were trying to get rid of him!"

"No!"

"You knew he'd come back!"

"That's not true!" she screamed, clapping her hands over her ears and rolling away from him.

He crossed the room to the bed. He picked the .38 out of the sheets.

"Where did you get this?"

When she didn't answer, he grabbed her arm and spun her around to him. "I said what the fuck are you doing with a gun!"

But he didn't wait for an explanation. He didn't want one. It didn't matter now. He dropped the pistol in the bottom drawer of the nightstand, then kicked it closed.

He walked back to stand over Tommy. He closed his eyes. He couldn't believe what had happened, what they'd done. He reached up and rubbed his temples with his fingertips, then took a deep breath and wiped both hands on his thighs.

He started toward the door. "You'd better get dressed," he said.

"Where are you going?" she asked, her voice rising in alarm.

"Where the hell do you think I'm going?"

"No!"

He stopped and turned around. "We don't have any choice."

"It was Tommy Gillespie," she cried. "That's all that's going to matter. Tommy's dead, and no one's going to care why. All they'll care is that I shot him."

"It was self-defense, Liana."

"They'll never believe that."

"You've got a witness," Cahill snapped, angry that she'd challenge him.

"What if they don't believe you either?"

Cahill had no intention of arguing further. He

started down the stairs. "That's a chance we'll just have to take," he said.

She ran after him. At the bottom of the stairs, he lifted the telephone receiver. As he dialed the operator, he turned and looked back up the stairs. She was on her knees at the bannister, the bedsheet wrapped around her shoulders like a shawl.

"People saw you," she cried. "People saw you and Tommy at the dance tonight. They saw it all. They saw what he did to you. You know what they'll think. They'll think you killed him. They'll think we killed him. They'll think the truth is just a story we made up to cover each other."

The operator came on the line. He pressed the receiver to his chest.

"Please, baby," she cried. "They'll never believe us, either of us."

He knew she was right.

He bent down behind Tommy and lifted him up to a sitting position, then slipped his arms around his waist and dragged him out onto the balcony. He hoisted him up onto the wrought-iron railing. Face down, the body folded neatly over it. As Liana stepped back out of the way, he reached down to Tommy's legs and then heaved him over.

With scarcely a sound, the body plunged headfirst into the darkness below, slipping through the glossy leaves of the camellias without snapping a single branch. It seemed to take forever for it to land on the pathway below. Then Tommy's skull clapped dully on the brick, like the thud of an axe into a round of oak.

Liana placed her hand on his forearm. Cahill tugged it away and she quickly stepped back, frightened by him.

"Do you want me to tell you I'm sorry?" she cried. "Well, I'm not. I had to do it. He would have killed you."

Cahill turned back to the railing and stared down through the camellias. She was right again. She had saved his life. He was alive, but he felt no relief, no redemption. He felt less delivered than merely spared.

"You'd have done the same for me," she said. "You'd have shot him, too. I know you would have."

She came up behind him, as close as a shadow. He pushed away from the railing and started toward the door.

"Get this cleaned up, then meet me out front," he said.

He walked downstairs and out the back of the house. Two feral cats had already discovered the body. They scattered reluctantly as Cahill approached.

He grabbed Tommy by the wrists and dragged him along the side of the house. His head rolled around his shoulders. The heels of his boots scraped across the brick.

When he reached the edge of the courtyard, he saw Tommy's pickup parked behind the Mustang, its polished fenders and chromed rims gleaming in the moonlight, and he realized they'd have to get rid of it too. He took a deep breath. He couldn't believe what they were doing, or what they were about to do.

He picked up Tommy's wrists again, then started toward the pickup. He felt exposed without the protection of the garden and hurried toward the truck. When he reached the pickup, he hoisted Tommy up. The body jackknifed forward, head and chest crashing heavily onto the tailgate, the truck sinking beneath his dead weight. He rolled Tommy into the bed, then slammed the tailgate.

He walked up to the cab and pulled the door open. At least the keys were in the ignition. The thought of having to search through Tommy's pockets gave him a chill.

As he pulled back out of the cab, Liana ran out the front door, then across the courtyard to him.

He handed her the keys to the Mustang. "Stay right behind me," he said. "We're going out to the river."

Crickets screeched in the dry grass along the edge of the dirt road, then fell silent as the pickup and then the Mustang rolled by. The pickup's tight coil springs creaked as they drove past the corral.

He turned down into the gully that ran along the Edison Canal. The headlights scissored through the dry brush. Jackrabbits bounded through the light, then disappeared into the brush.

Then he realized they couldn't dump Tommy into the river with the truck. Suddenly it seemed so obvious. It worried him that he hadn't realized that immediately. There were too many complications.

A half-mile down the canal he pulled in beneath the dark, tar-soaked timbers of the railroad trestle that spanned the canal. As the Mustang pulled in behind him, he climbed out of the cab and started back to the car.

Liana doused the headlights, then killed the engine. "What are we doing here?" she asked.

"There's a rope in the trunk," he said. "Bring it."

He returned to the truck and dropped the tailgate, then he rolled Tommy onto the ground.

"I thought we were headed out to the river," she said behind him.

"We can't just dump Tommy and his truck in the river," he snapped, as if it had been her idea instead of his. "You think that'd be the end of it? What happens when they find his body? What happens when they see he's been shot?"

"I don't know," she retreated.

"There's no way we can hide the truck. No

matter what we do with it, they're gonna find it. But maybe if we're lucky we can keep them from finding Tommy's body."

She didn't say anything.

He slammed the tailgate closed, then waded down to the foot of the trestle. He climbed over the broken slabs of concrete until he found a piece he could move. He dug his fingers into the dirt beneath it until he gained a solid grip, then he pulled up the slab so that he could roll it up the bank.

The slab was nearly too heavy. He spent as much of his strength balancing it as he did pushing it through the grass and up the bank and then across the trestle. But he knew that a piece too light was worth nothing.

Finally he worked the concrete out to the center of the span. Then he dragged Tommy out to the middle of the trestle and laid him down beside the slab.

"Give me the rope," he said, and Liana handed it to him without a word.

"You can go back to the car," he said, but she didn't move and he didn't argue with her.

He tied Tommy to the slab, binding his wrists and ankles together, then lashing the rope around the concrete and his chest. He cinched the rope as tight as he could, then added a final knot.

Then he rolled him off the edge of the trestle. The body splashed through the surface, then sank to the bottom in a fountain of air bubbles. They watched the canal until the bubbles stopped, praying the body wasn't rising with them.

CHAPTER 7

Cahill gunned the engine and turned up the bank. The pickup crashed through the Johnson grass and pulled onto River Road. He stopped and waited for Liana. Only a second passed before the Mustang roared up behind him.

He slipped the pickup into gear and headed down the road, a thin, seldom-traveled ribbon of asphalt that wound through the rice and sorghum and safflower fields along the east bank of the river. Soon it began to follow the Sacramento, riding up onto the levees, tunneling through the walnut and almond orchards that crowded up to its banks, skirting the fields that fanned out below.

In a few minutes, he spotted the yellow-and-black sign he was looking for. Peppered with a tight pattern of holes from a shotgun blast, it warned that the road veered sharply to the right. Years ago the road had followed the sweeping rim of a broad oxbow bend in the river, but the winter floodwaters had swallowed the bank so frequently that the stretch of road had come to be known as the Washout. Now the pavement ended abruptly, and a temporary road angled hard to the north.

Once or twice a year, a drunk rancher or maybe a carload of farmworkers missed the turn and plunged over the bank. This time Tommy would be the unfortunate victim. When the truck was spotted, the sheriff would send in divers and they'd begin dragging the river. But they could search every slough and back eddy from the Washout to the Delta, and they'd never find him. It was their only chance.

Without a body, the sheriff would have to assume Tommy had drowned. He'd learn Tommy'd been drinking all day at the picnic. He'd remember the time Tommy lost control of his Camaro and spun off into an orchard. He'd have to believe Tommy was driving too fast and drove off into the river. There would be no other assumption to make, no other conclusion to draw.

Cahill pulled over to the shoulder. While Liana eased in behind him, he studied the road as it ran toward the river, then climbed the levee. A shallow orchard ditch ran along the left side of the road. On the right was a dilapidated sheet metal pumphouse.

"This is it," he said to Liana, who had walked up to the cab of the truck.

"What about you?"

He looked through the window at her. "I

thought I'd jump out before it goes into the drink," he said.

She managed a dismal smile. "It sounds like you've thought of everything."

She stepped back out of the way as he slipped the truck into gear and guided it back onto the pavement. He shifted through second into third. The truck surged down the middle of the road and began hurtling toward the river. His stomach tightened as he opened the door and moved out onto the running board, clinging to the steering wheel through the open window. He squinted ahead, into the mosquitoes and black flies swarming through the headlights. To keep the truck from veering off the road, he had to stay with it as long as he could.

Suddenly he felt it sweep up the back of the levee. The truck rose up beneath him like a horse breaking into a run. He leapt clear and could feel himself cartwheeling through the darkness. He could smell the river. He could hear the engine howl.

First her eyes, remote and distant, then the gentle lines of her face swam into focus. He could feel her soft hands on his cheeks. He tried to sit up but could barely lift his head. He immediately fell back down and could feel her gathering him in her arms, cradling him like a child.

The words rushed out of her all at once. "You were perfect, baby. You were perfect," she said. "You were driving down the road and then all of a sudden you were flying clear of the truck. But then I couldn't find you. I was calling your name but you didn't answer, and then when I found you I thought you'd broken your neck."

"I'm all right," he said.

He rolled out of her lap and pushed up onto his hands and knees, then tried to straighten up, rising to his feet as tentatively as if he were balancing on a wire.

He waited for the pain. He hurt all over. Suddenly he felt himself reeling. He reached out for Liana and caught her shoulder, then leaned forward and touched the back of his head. He could feel the blood matting his hair. He wondered how long he'd been unconscious.

"Let's go, baby," she said as he draped an arm around her neck.

They waded back through the tules, fighting their way down the silty ditch bottom until they found a spot to climb out. Liana went first. As Cahill leaned against the bank he could hear the Mustang idling evenly on the road. For an instant a wave of nausea rolled over him. He thought he might even faint, but then it passed.

"Here," she said.

She reached down to him, and then he felt her pulling him up by the collar of his shirt.

"We've got to make sure the truck made it into the river," he said.

He leaned forward, his hands on his knees.

"I'm all right," he insisted. "We've got to check."

She slipped her arm around his waist, and they walked up the road to the top of the levee. They gazed down at the river. The moonlight glistened on the metallic, blue-black surface. He could hear the current playing on the far shore. There was no sign of the truck.

He took a deep breath, as if the cool air moving down the river could give him strength. He wanted to believe they were done with Tommy, but he knew the current would carry the truck downriver. By morning it would wash up onto the long, cobbled spit of gravel less than a hundred yards downriver and someone would spot it. That's when it would all begin.

"Let's get the hell out of here," he said.

Cahill ran the faucet in the bathroom sink, then bent down and splashed his face with cold water. When he straightened up, Liana was in the mirror behind him, her white robe loosely closed.

"Let me see," she said.

He braced himself on the sink.

"Hold still," she instructed him.

She clipped the hair away from the loose flap of scalp, then cleaned out the wound with a warm, wet cloth and dressed it with a pad of gauze.

"I think you're going to live," she said, and

then she turned and moved back into the bedroom.

His vision was still slightly doubled. He studied himself in the mirror. Lines radiated from the corners of his eyes. The stubble that shadowed his jaw was flecked with gray. The thin crescent of a scar high on his right cheekbone, won years ago in a desultory brawl at the county fair, had nearly dissolved into memory.

He reached up and parted his hair with his fingertips. There was no concealing the bandage. Sooner or later he was going to have to explain it, and that was going to mean explaining where he'd been all night.

He pulled open the door of the medicine cabinet. A row of plastic prescription bottles lined the bottom shelf. He found a bottle of Darvon and swallowed two of them to still the pounding at the back of his head.

He returned to the bedroom. Liana was in bed, leaning back against two pillows pushed up against the bed frame, the pale yellow sheet clutched beneath her chin.

"I never meant for this to happen," she said. "When Faith called and told me you were home, I didn't want to go to the picnic with Tommy. I wanted to see you.

"Then once we got to the picnic, all I did was look for you. Finally I saw Faith and David Earle dancing, and then I saw you. Tommy was talking to some people. I didn't think he'd even notice I was gone."

Cahill picked a cigarette from a pack on the vanity, then broke off the filter and pinched it into the corner of his mouth. He knew the cigarettes were Tommy's, but he didn't care.

"He noticed, all right," he said as he struck a match.

She brushed her hair back off her forehead. "He was furious on the ride back here, but I didn't care. I thought when I told him I felt sick he'd know I didn't want to see him and just leave. I didn't care that he was mad. He was always mad about something.

"Then I drove into town looking for you."

He crossed the room and stood in the open balcony doors. The dark fields rolled out across the floor of the valley like a smooth, black tropical bay. He could smell the fermenting soil and water. The sky was beginning to lighten. It was almost day.

"They're going to know you were the last one to see Tommy," he said. "As soon as they find his truck, they're gonna come out here."

"I'll tell the truth," she said. "I'll tell them Tommy and I went to the picnic and stayed for the fireworks and then the dance. I'll tell them I wasn't feeling well, so Tommy brought me home. That was maybe eleven o'clock. I'll tell them I never saw him after that."

Cahill took a deep breath; he winced as a shaft of pain drove through his head. "I wouldn't exactly call that the truth."

"It's close enough."

"Don't tell them you drove into town look-ing for me. You can't let them know I came out here."

"You make it sound so wrong."

"You know how it would look."

"I know, I know," she said. "I'll keep you out of it."

He turned around to her. She ran her hands over her bare arms as if she were chilled.

"I'll get you something to help you sleep," he said.

He gave her a Valium. She chased it with a shot of brandy.

He set the snifter on the nightstand, then sat down beside her. She rolled her head into his lap.

"I've got to go," he said.

She abruptly pulled back away from him. "Now?"

"That's right," he said.

"Please, baby. You can't go. Don't leave me alone."

"I have to."

"You're leaving, aren't you—like last time. This is it, isn't it? I'll never see you again."

"No, Liana," he said, reaching out and tak-ing her by the shoulders. "I'll be back."

"How do I know?" she cried.

"You've got my word."

"How do I know for sure?"

He took a deep breath.
"That's the best I can do, Liana."

He walked downstairs, then out of the house. He hated to leave her; he hated to leave her alone. But he couldn't stay. The risk was simply too great that someone would see him or notice his car. Already the sky was paling from black to blue.

He slipped into the Mustang and headed back out to the Midway. It was lunacy to believe they could get away with what they'd done. Now there was nothing to do but wait—and hope against hope that things fell their way.

CHAPTER 8

FLOODING INTO THE bedroom, the flat midday sun blinded him. From a deep, dreamless sleep, Cahill raised himself up onto his elbows, but the instant he realized where he was—and what they'd done the night before—he dropped back onto the mattress and stared up at the ceiling.

After a minute he rolled out of bed and pulled on his jeans. The house was hot. He made his way around the living room, closing the windows and drawing the shades, then he turned on the swamp cooler. It rumbled and groaned and then a blast of moist air blew into the room.

He walked into the kitchen and put a saucepan of water on the back burner, then took down a jar of instant coffee from the cabinet. The clock on the wall above the refrigerator said it was almost four in the afternoon. At first he couldn't believe he'd slept through the day. Then he realized it must have been the Darvon.

He wondered if the Valium was still working on Liana. He wondered what she was doing. It worried him that she was alone.

Suddenly the screen door slammed and Faith rushed into the kitchen.

"Did you hear about Tommy? He's dead! He drove his truck into the river and drowned himself!"

She was breathing hard. "When I saw it in the newspaper, all I could think was that Liana had drowned too. It happened last night—after the dance out at Hudson Grove. All I could think was that Liana might have been in the truck too and maybe nobody knew it.

"I called out to the ranch, and no one answered. The phone rang and rang, and I thought, my God, it's true. I was going out of my mind."

She took a deep breath. "Finally Liana answered the phone. She said she'd been out at the corral, but I know she was there in the house. I know she just wasn't answering. I didn't know whether to kill her or just be glad she's all right."

She looked at him for a second, then spun around to the sink. She ran the tap, then cupped her hand and raised the water to her mouth. He could hear her drinking as quietly as a cat.

He spooned the instant coffee into a white porcelain cup.

"What else did she say?" he asked.

"What do you mean?"

"Did she know about Tommy?"

"Of course she knew. Everyone knows."

She pushed away from the sink and stepped up behind him. "What the hell did you do to your head?"

Suddenly his face felt like it was on fire.

"This?" he asked, reaching up and gingerly touching the pad of gauze.

"What do you think I'm talking about?"

His mind wheeled. He couldn't tell her the truth. He laughed nervously.

"I met a woman down at the Blue Orchid last night."

Faith looked at him for a second, then shook her head and lifted the gauze to inspect the wound. "Don't tell me it was true love."

"She wanted to get a motel room. It seemed like a good idea at the time."

"A motel room?"

"The Thunderbird."

"She must have been married."

Cahill nodded. "To an Indian," she said. "She was pissed off at him."

"This is rich."

"You don't believe me?"

Faith pressed the gauze back in place. Her face threatened a smile.

"Oh, I believe you, Winn. Why shouldn't I believe you? All your life you've never been anything but straight with me, right?"

He shrugged, couldn't help but laugh.

"So what did she do to your head?"

"Well, the minute we stepped into the room, she tells me she wants to take a shower. I said go on ahead, but then she says she means the both of us. She wants me in the shower too."

"Maybe I don't want to hear the rest of this," Faith said.

"Right away she started getting romantic. You wouldn't believe what that woman could do with a bar of soap."

"That's enough," Faith said, glaring at him.

"I mean we were in a lather from head to toe."

She turned and started for the front door. "I've got better things to do than listen to you brag about some tramp you wise-talked into bed."

Cahill followed her through the house.

"Pretty quick I've got her up against the tile. The water's drilling me in the back. She's got her legs wrapped around my waist."

"I said that's enough!" Faith shouted back over her shoulder, but Cahill had no intention of letting up.

"All of a sudden we're crashing through the shower curtain. The next thing I knew, I was lying there buck naked on the bathroom floor. I must have hit my head on the sink."

Faith stopped and spun back around to him. "You're still a jerk, aren't you, Winn? You're still a real blue-ribbon jerk."

"You wanted to know," he said.

She drove off without so much as a wave or a glance.

The instant her blue Falcon turned the corner, he leapt behind the wheel of the Mustang, then raced down to Fulton's Market just two blocks away.

He pulled up in front of the small neighborhood grocery, then ran up to the yellow newspaper box standing beside the door. When he saw the newspaper in the window of the box, he felt like he'd been kicked in the chest.

Splashed across the front page was a photograph of Tommy's pickup being hauled up out of the river. Two tow trucks were backed up to the edge of the bank, winching the truck up on taut steel cables. The windshield had shattered. A dense web of cracks ran through the glass.

He shoved his hands deep into his pockets, but he didn't have any change. He'd left his wallet back at the old man's house. He glanced into the store, then placed a hand on the newspaper box handle. With all his weight he wrenched it down and then swung the door open, then he snatched a paper from inside and hustled back to the car.

He unfolded the front page. In another photograph, a man Cahill knew to be Steven Coles, who owned the marina at Eden's Landing, was directing the recovery operation from a flat-bottomed outboard, the Evinrude clamped to its transom holding the skiff steady in the current. Two divers in dark wetsuits watched on from the edge of the water. At the top of the bank stood Kevin Mooney, the sheriff, his arms folded across his tan uniform.

At the bottom of the page was a photograph of Tommy, taken from the high school yearbook. Thick muttonchop sideburns grew down the sides of his face. Inside the collar of his shirt a shark's tooth on a silver chain lay on his pallid skin.

Cahill flung the paper into the back seat, then started up the Mustang and took off.

He found Liana on the terrace, stretched out on a lounge chair beside the pool. She was wearing a blue nylon one-piece swimsuit. Water from the pool still glistened on her skin. Beside her, on a white wire-mesh table, was a glass of wine and a bowl of grapes.

He walked out onto the terrace. She spun around to him when she heard his footsteps on the red tile behind her. Clutching her hands to her chest, she took a deep breath.

"You startled me."

He dropped the newspaper onto the table, upsetting the glass of wine. It splashed through the mesh onto the tile.

Liana glanced down at the front page, then looked back up at him.

"I know," she said. "Faith told me."

He sat down.

"Faith said you weren't answering the phone."

"I finally answered," she said.

"Who did you think it was gonna be?"

"I don't know," she said. "I don't know what you mean."

Cahill gazed past her. The surface of the pool was as still and tense as glass.

"Have you talked to Tommy's father?"

"No," she said.

"Why not?"

"Why?"

"Your boyfriend just drowned in the river, Liana. You're supposed to be consumed with grief. You act like you're on vacation."

"He wasn't my boyfriend," she said softly, but Cahill wasn't listening.

"What the fuck is Mooney gonna think if he comes out here and finds you lying by the pool?"

She stared at him a moment. "What do you want me to do?"

"Make the fucking call!"

He waited for her on the terrace. A heavy silence had descended on the valley. He could feel it pressing down on him.

After a few minutes she walked back out of the house. He turned around to her.

"What did he say?"

She shook her head. "I talked to Miranda. Mooney had been there. She said Calvin had been drinking. He couldn't talk to anyone right now."

Cahill took a deep breath.

"I'm sorry," she said. "I know I should have done it sooner."

She came to him and slipped her arms around his waist, pressing her head against his chest. "Come inside for a minute," she said. "I want to show you something."

"Do you remember these?"

She handed him two black-and-white snapshots.

"Faith took them," she said.

In the first he was standing on stage at the Silver Dollar fairgrounds; he was playing with the Wheels, his Stratocaster riding low on his hip, his long black hair flowing out from beneath the black Stetson Liana had given him on his twenty-first birthday. In the second, he and Liana were leaning back against the Mustang, her head on his shoulder, his arm slipped around her back. He couldn't believe how young they looked, how much time had been lost.

Liana took the photographs back from him. She studied them for a minute, then turned away and carried the photographs over to the vanity, where she tucked them inside the mirror frame.

He sat down in the wicker chair across the room, watching as she withdrew a simple white dress from the closet. A pattern of small red roses ran through the soft cloth. She slipped it off the hanger and then held it beneath her chin, clutching it to her body in front of the vanity's mirror, swaying softly to the radio.

"This used to be your favorite," she said. She glanced up into the mirror and smiled at him. "There wasn't a time I wore this dress that some purely depraved notion didn't creep into your head."

He watched her lay the dress on the bed, then she crossed the room to him and turned her back. She shrugged out of the swimsuit, stooping to pull it down and then kicking it away.

Then she picked the dress off the bed and slipped it over her head. She performed a slow pirouette, her hands above her head, the dress lifting off her legs.

She smiled. "It still fits," she said. "See, I haven't changed so much."

Then she paused to study herself in the mirror. She turned sideways to examine her profile. She cupped her breasts in her hands, then inhaled deeply, filling her lungs with air.

"I was always worried about my boobs," she said. "They're not the same size. They're uneven. The left one is bigger." She caught his eye in the mirror. "Faith used to tell me it was because I had a big heart."

Cahill didn't say anything.

She crossed the room and knelt down before him and rested her head on the top of his knee.

"Don't go cold on me, Winn Cahill—not now. We'll be all right," she said. "You'll see."

* * *

He stood on the balcony. She walked out behind him.

Thunderclouds were stacking up above the Coast Range. The wind had begun to rise in the south. The change in direction was as unmistakable as it was unusual. Rain was coming.

Liana slipped her arm through his and pressed up against him. "We didn't do anything that was so terrible," she said. "We didn't do anything wrong. All we wanted was to be together. What's so terrible about that?

"Maybe you were right. Maybe we should have called the sheriff. But he wouldn't have believed us—ever. Why should we have to pay for something we didn't mean to do? Tommy would have killed you, and then he would have killed me. We didn't have any choice."

Cahill took a deep breath. "I know, Liana. I know."

CHAPTER 9

WHEN HE GOT back to the old man's house, he rolled a joint and sat at the dining room table. He turned on the radio. On a call-in talkshow, a woman from Las Vegas claimed she'd seen Howard Hughes buying a Cadillac at a used car lot in Phoenix. He listened for another hour, but then the callers began to depress him. At midnight he turned on the television and dropped down onto the sofa to watch the all-night westerns.

Finally he fell asleep. He didn't wake until he heard a car door slam in front of the house. An afternoon soap was playing on the television.

He rose from the sofa and peered out the front window. Mooney was standing beside the Mustang in the driveway. Cahill's throat tightened; he tried to swallow through it.

Mooney was a tall, solid man with hooded eyes and a wide, thick-lipped mouth. His uniform was stretched across his chest as taut as if it had been fashioned of wet leather. The

sleeves were rolled up as tight as seams, gir-
dling his veined biceps. He wore the badge on
his chest like a medal won in combat.

Cahill could feel the sweat beading up around
his mouth. Mooney knew he was there. There
was nowhere to hide, no way to run. He had
no choice but to summon his nerve and pushed
out through the screen door.

"Afternoon, Winn," Mooney said as Cahill
stepped out onto the porch.

Mooney walked up to the house. Cahill met
him at the bottom of the steps, and they shook
hands.

"I heard you were back in town," he said.

Cahill nodded cautiously. "It's been a couple
days now," he said.

Mooney reached into his shirt pocket and
produced a pack of cigarettes. He shook one
out of the pack and tapped the tobacco down
against his thick yellow thumbnail. Cahill
watched him take it between his teeth, then flip
back the lid of a chrome lighter and raise the
blue flame to light it.

"Listen, Winn," he said. "You hear we
found Tommy Gillespie's pickup in the river
yesterday?"

"I read about it."

Mooney nodded, then slipped his lighter
back into his pants. "I understand you and
Tommy had a few words out at Hudson Grove
the other night—that's the reason I ask."

"Liana Harris and I danced together. Tommy didn't take kindly to it."

"That's it?"

"That's it," Cahill said. "Sorry to disappoint you."

Mooney took a long drag on his cigarette. "Oh, I'm not disappointed, Winn. But I can understand a man getting upset when another man asks his woman to dance, can't you?"

"I wouldn't exactly call her Tommy's woman," Cahill said.

Mooney shrugged. "Maybe you're right," he said. "She was yours once, wasn't she, Winn?"

"That was a long time ago," Cahill said.

Mooney smiled. "And I'll bet you never give those days a moment's thought, do you?"

Cahill stared at him.

"Do you mind if I ask what you did after the dance?" Mooney asked.

"I went down to the Blue Orchid."

"You were there until it closed?"

"That's right."

"And then you came here?"

"Not exactly," he said. He tried to remember the story he'd given Faith.

"What does that mean?"

"I met a woman," he said.

"Does this woman have a name?"

"What does her name matter?" Cahill asked. "I don't see any reason to drag her into this."

"Into what, Winn?"

"Into whatever this is."

"Was she married?"

"She might have been. She said she was."

Mooney studied Cahill for a second, then nodded to himself, thinking it over.

"Do you mind if I ask what you and this woman did? If she was married, I don't guess you took her back to her place. I figure you're smarter than that."

Cahill smiled at him. "You give me too much credit."

"I figure you for a smart guy, Winn. Did you bring her here?"

"We went to a motel," he said, but the instant he said it he realized he'd made a terrible mistake.

"What motel?"

"What does any of this have to do with finding Tommy's truck in the goddamn river?" he snapped.

It took Mooney by surprise. He watched Cahill closely for a second.

"I'm just trying to find out what happened to Tommy the other night," he said. "Liana told me Tommy took her home after the dance. She said she thought Tommy was headed home. I'm just trying to figure out what he was doing out at the river."

"How the hell am I supposed to know what Tommy was doing out there?"

Mooney studied him a second, then flicked his cigarette over his shoulder. It landed in the uncut grass, trailing a string of smoke.

"Well, I guess you don't," Mooney said, and shrugged. "I made a mistake, Winn. I guess I'm just wasting your time."

He turned and started back to his car, pausing to grind out the cigarette with the toe of his boot. Then he glanced back up at Cahill.

"What did you do to your head? You don't mind telling me that, do you?"

Cahill laughed, louder than he knew he should have. "I slipped in the shower," he said.

"No," Mooney said.

"It's the truth."

"Sounds like you're accident-prone, Winn. You'd better be careful now, you hear what I'm telling you?"

"I'll try to watch myself."

Mooney smiled. "Just one last thing, Winn."

"What's that?"

"What was the name of that motel?"

Cahill walked down the hall on the third floor of the Woodrow Building. He opened the frosted glass door to Wagner's office and leaned inside. Rosa, Wagner's secretary, was reading a supermarket tabloid spread out on the desk before her.

She looked up reluctantly. She had long black hair and skin the color of polished walnut. Her red fingernails were curved like claws.

"I'm looking for David Earle," he said.

"He's in conference."

"It's important."

Brushing her forehead with the back of her hand, she said, "I'm sure it is. It's always important."

"Is he in the office?"

She arched an eyebrow.

"How long will he be in conference?"

"I couldn't say."

"This won't take but a minute," Cahill said, walking past her desk to the door to Wagner's office.

"Wait!" she called out to him, but by the time she rose from her chair he had already let himself in.

Wagner sat at a desk buried beneath stacks of court documents and file folders. His boots were kicked up onto the corner of the desk. Despite the small electric fan laboring in the window, the smell of marijuana permeated the room. A half-smoked joint lay on a bed of spent matches in a glass ashtray in front of him.

"I see you're hard at work," Cahill said.

Wagner smiled at him. His eyes were red and reduced to slits. "The defense never rests," he said.

He looked over to Rosa, standing in the doorway behind Cahill. "It's all right," he said. "I can handle him. I'll call if I need the heavy artillery."

Cahill glanced at her. She glared at him, then backed out of the room.

"And hold my calls!" Wagner shouted through the closed door.

Wagner rocked forward in his chair, then withdrew a bottle of tequila and two shotglasses from the bottom drawer of his desk.

"You've upset her, Winn. You should have made an appointment. We might have avoided the histrionics."

Cahill walked over to the window and looked down through the blinds at the boarded-up storefronts and the steel grates covering the windows of a pawnshop. At the mouth of the alley that ran behind Cutter's Café a young Mexican in a white apron leaned back against the brick wall beneath a hand-painted sign on the wall above him that advertised Wine by the Glass.

"I'm in trouble," he said.

"Lucky for you, Winn, I specialize in trouble." Wagner filled the shotglasses with tequila. "You've only been home three days. How much trouble can you be in?"

Cahill wondered if talking to Wagner wasn't a mistake. He didn't know what he expected Wagner to do. But he didn't know where else to turn.

"I drove out to the Harris ranch the other night," he said.

Wagner laughed. "I wonder why," he said, and then he threw back one of the shotglasses.

"This was after the dance, after that ridiculous scene with Tommy. First I went down to the Blue Orchid. When I got back to the old man's place, there was a note from Liana telling me to come out to see her. I figured what the hell. It was late. I didn't get out there until maybe three in the morning."

Wagner let his breath out through his teeth. "This is the night Tommy took the big swim?"

Cahill closed his eyes. He could see Tommy standing in the doorway, his gaunt face lit by the flare of the match; he could hear Liana screaming.

"Liana told him she was feeling sick. He left, and then she drove into town and left a note for me on the old man's door. She didn't know where Tommy went. She didn't care.

"Well the son of a bitch came back out to the ranch. He found me and Liana in her bedroom. He went crazy. He started beating on her. When I tried to stop him, he pulled a knife on me. I swear to God I thought I was dead."

Cahill turned away from the window. Wagner was watching him. "Then Liana shot him."

Wagner rocked forward in his chair; his boots clapped on the linoleum floor. "What the fuck are you talking about?"

Cahill shook his head. "We dumped his body in the Edison Canal, then we dumped the truck into the river to make it look like an accident."

"Are you out of your fucking mind?" Wagner shouted.

But then Wagner stopped, pulling himself back. He took a deep breath, then motioned to the chair in front of his desk. "Sit down, Winn," he said.

After a second, Cahill crossed the room and dropped into the chair. A long silence enveloped them.

"Why didn't you tell me?" Wagner asked.

"I didn't know what the fuck to do. All I knew was Mooney wasn't going to believe us no matter what we told him. She shot the son of a bitch in the back. How the hell were we going to explain that?"

Wagner rubbed his eyes with his fingertips. "Jesus Christ," he sighed.

He put his glasses back on. "How is Liana handling this?"

"She's all right."

Wagner shook his head. "Of course she is," he said to himself. "You two are perfect, Winn. You're absolutely perfect for each other. You always were."

CHAPTER 10

STORM CLOUDS BULLED over the coast range and across the valley. Down the road leading into the ranch, a frond broke off one of the palms and crashed to the ground. A lone western gull, driven inland by the winds, shrieked and circled overhead.

Cahill walked up to the house. He let himself in and called Liana's name, but there was no answer, so he moved out onto the patio in back. He looked up at the balcony off her bedroom, but no lights were on.

He skirted the edge of the pool and walked out the gate in the wall that surrounded the house. In the deepening dusk a pickup was slowly making its way in from the back of the ranch, its headlights kicking up as the truck lurched down the rutted road. He took a slug from the half-pint of tequila he'd bought after leaving Wagner's office, then shoved it into his back pocket.

He waited for the truck to reach the house. A wave of dust washed over him as it came to a stop. In the glare of the headlights he still couldn't see who it was, but he knew it had to be Cassidy, Liana's foreman, who must have been checking the water in the rice fields.

With the engine idling, the door opened, and Cassidy slid out from behind the wheel. He was a thin, frail man with a lean face, sallow skin and gold wire-rimmed glasses. In creased khakis and a flannel shirt buttoned snugly at the collar, he looked more like a minister than the foreman of the ranch.

"Is there something I can do for you?" Cassidy asked.

"I'm looking for Liana," Cahill said.

Cassidy took off his glasses, then began cleaning the lenses with a neatly folded handkerchief. "She never said nothing to me about anyone coming out to see her."

"Everyone who wants to see her checks in with you?"

"It's not such a bad idea," Cassidy said. "This is private property. I don't know you from the criminal element."

Cahill smiled, then raised both arms as if he were under arrest. "Do I look like a criminal?"

But Cassidy didn't bite. He put his glasses back on, then replaced the handkerchief in his shirt pocket. "You got a name?"

"I'm an old friend," Cahill said.

"Is that right," Cassidy said. "Well, I hope so, friend, because if I find out any different we'll talk again, and you won't enjoy our conversation a bit.''

Then Cassidy climbed back into the truck and slammed the door.

"You'll find her out at the corral," he said, and then he ground the truck into gear and slowly headed out to the Midway.

Cahill watched him go. As the taillights died out into the distance he couldn't help but wonder why Cassidy had stood by while his wife fled back to their native Missouri. There had to be a reason Cassidy couldn't convince her that Lillian Harris's wild accusations were simply the lunatic ravings of a grieving old woman. There had to be a reason he'd stayed.

Liana was standing in the middle of the corral. In front of her an unsaddled palomino reared onto its back legs, kicking its forelegs in front of its chest. Liana jumped to the side and tugged down hard on the reins, but the palomino reared away from her again, jerking the reins out of her hands and then bolting across the corral.

She turned when she sensed Cahill approaching, then slipped through the fence and draped her arms over the top rail. The palomino angrily stamped the ground, then threw its head back and bared its teeth.

"You've got a new horse," he said.

"His name is Sonny," she said. "The storm has him spooked."

"Whatever happened to Highway?"

"He got star-thistle poisoning," she said. "I had to have Cassidy shoot him. It was horrible."

Cahill pulled the half-pint from his back pocket and took a sip. "That's too bad," he said.

He offered the half-pint to Liana, but she shook her head. He watched as she moved back out to the palomino. She approached him slowly, her hand extended. The palomino's stringy tail whipped across its haunches; its head angled up at the sky. But it didn't back away. She reached for the reins lying across its broad neck. Swiftly, expertly, she removed the bridle and bit.

"You told Mooney about the dance," he said as she hung the bridle on a spike driven into the wall of the stable. "You told him Tommy and I got into an argument."

"He would have found out sooner or later," she said.

She turned back to him, then slapped the dust out of her jeans. "How would it have looked if I'd pretended it hadn't happened, if I'd ignored it altogether? He'd have known I was hiding something from him."

Cahill took a breath, then let it out slowly. He supposed Liana was right. Still, it unnerved him. He didn't like her talking to Mooney. There was no way to know what she might say.

"What did he want?" she asked.

"He wanted to knew where I went after the dance."

"What did you tell him?"

"I told him I went down to the Blue Orchid. I told him I met a woman there."

"He won't have any trouble believing that."

"He wanted to know what we did and where we went."

She looked at him. Cahill laughed. "I told him we went out to the Thunderbird Motel."

"What if he checks?"

"He'll check," he said. "And the minute he does, he'll know I was lying through my teeth."

Ligtning vaulted across the sky. In the sudden flash of light the long train of palms leading out to the midway looked skeletal and frail.

Thunder detonated overhead. Standing on the balcony off Liana's bedroom, Cahill could feel the concussion in his chest. Then the rain began.

"A man came by one day and said he wanted to buy all the palm trees," Liana said.

She turned and looked at him. "He wanted to dig them up and then take them down to Los Angeles. They plant them around shopping malls."

She reached out over the balcony railing until the rain pouring off the roof splashed into her hand.

"Did you like living there?" she asked.

"I made some good friends," he said after a moment's hesitation.

"Were any of them women?"

He thought for a minute and could see Darlene asleep on the couch, the room lit only by the television. He remembered the night he met her at the gas station, the steaks they barbecued in the middle of the night, the champagne they drank; he remembered her undisciplined voice and the dream she once had of becoming a singer. It made him sad, though he didn't know exactly why.

"One was," he said.

"Was she important to you?"

"I never married her, if that's what you mean."

She pulled her hand back in from the rain.

"Are you going back to her?"

"First I just want to get out of here," he said.

She moved over to him. She stood behind him and slipped a hand through his open shirt, then ran it up and across his chest, pressing her head against the back of his shoulder.

"They can't prove anything," she said.

Another bolt of lightning split the sky. Thunder rocked the house. The windows rattled in their iron frames. The light in the bedroom dimmed, and then the house fell dark.

"Do you remember the trip we took to Mexico?" she asked.

He pulled the half-pint out of his pocket and took a sip.

"Do you remember the old beach hotel in Rosarito?"

She let go of him and walked back to the railing. She gazed out into the storm. "I know you do," she said.

Then she turned back around to him. "That's what we should do," she said. "We should just pick up and go to Mexico. I'll sell the ranch. We'll just disappear."

"I don't think so, Liana."

"But it's a thought, isn't it?"

"I suppose."

"They say it's the thought that counts."

She returned to him, then rose up onto her toes and kissed his neck; she ran her fingers across his bare chest. "There's another thought coming to me right now," she said.

He didn't resist her as she closed her mouth over his.

With the electricity out, the clock had stopped. Cahill had no idea how long he'd been watching her sleep. She scarcely moved. In the warm, luxuriant darkness she lay on her back, hands folded neatly across her stomach as if she were reposing in a coffin.

He couldn't believe she owned the Harris ranch now. It made him want to laugh. He could imagine how that ate at the good citizens of Loma Roja—how deeply they resented her, how willingly they believed she was involved in Michael's death.

Her mother was a tall, raven-haired woman who wore rings on all her fingers and dozens of metal bracelets on her wrists. She had black piercing eyes and favored dark purple lipstick. Her name was Clarisse, and in the late afternoon, after several glasses of the red wine they bottled in the basement, she liked to boast she could read the future in the lines of your palm. Liana's father was a thin, stoop-shouldered man everyone called Lucky for the slug he'd taken in the groin in the Second World War. Although the wound left him with a severe limp, two inches to the right would have made a world of difference.

They had a small ranch some thirty miles south of town—261 acres of marsh and sink along Holmes Creek. They tried to make a go of it planting corn and safflower and beans on the dry ground, but over the years they fell increasingly in debt. When Liana was in the seventh grade, the Baldwin Land Company offered what seemed on paper like a fair price for the ranch. Though it was still scarcely enough to pay their outstanding bills, they were facing foreclosure and had no choice but to sell and move into town.

The land company had little interest in the low, badly draining ranch. What it wanted were the rights the ranch held to a share of Holmes Creek. That water could be diverted to the Vincent ranch, one of the company's largest rice operations, which the land company was hav-

ing to flood with water pumped from under-
ground aquifers. To the attorneys in the
company's corporate headquarters, high in a
glass-and-steel tower in San Francisco's finan-
cial district, the acquisition was no more than a
sound business move. The cost of purchasing
the Blake ranch would be recovered by not having to run the pumps at the Vincent ranch.

The first winter after the sale, a group of land
company attorneys came up to the ranch to
hunt the duck and geese that came down into
marshes along the creek. The first night they
were there a fire broke out in the flue of the
wood stove. By the time the neighboring ranchers arrived, the house was completely engulfed
in flames. There was nothing they could do as
the roof beams collapsed and clouds of sparks
and embers sailed up into the night. They could
only watch as the drunken attorneys howled
and cheered and hurled bottles through the
windows. Now all that remained of the house
where Liana had been born were the scorched
stone walls and the water tower still standing
behind it on tall, stilted legs, its disconnected
pipes jutting into the air. The ground had lain
fallow for years.

Her father never got over losing the ranch.
Although he found work as a mechanic at the
Ford garage, he soon fell hard into the bottle.
He and Liana's mother began to quarrel. Their
fights grew bitter and occasionally violent, until
finally he stopped coming home at all. Then

one night he stole a red Fairlane from the Ford garage and took off. Several days later the car was found abandoned in Reno. As far as Cahill knew, Liana hadn't seen her father since.

Although her mother never remarried, she eventually took up with a man named Lester Sheen. Sheen was a wildcatter, a sturdy, barrel-chested man who made a living drilling gas wells. Whenever Cahill saw him, Sheen was either dead broke or flush with crisp new twenty-dollar bills he liked to snap with his fingers. He did most of his work down in Texas and along the Gulf Coast, but he called on Clarisse every time he came through the valley.

Once, while assembling a new group of investors to put down a well on the west side of the river, Sheen stayed with Clarisse for several months. Cahill and Liana were living out on Kingdom Road at the time, and Clarisse seemed buoyed by Sheen's presence in the house. But then the new well failed to tap any gas, and when the investors learned there was no money to drill any deeper, Sheen prudently decided to return to Texas. Clarisse went with him.

That was all the family Liana had ever had. First they'd lost their ranch. Now her father was wanted on stolen-car charges, her mother by those investors whose savings her boyfriend had sunk down a dry hole. Cahill shook his head, then reached over to the vanity for the cigarettes Tommy had left. He shook one out of the pack, lit it. Maybe Liana just had bad blood. Maybe it was just that simple.

He remembered the day he first met her. It was years ago—a blistering summer afternoon while they were still in high school. He and Wagner had decided to drive out to the Western Canal for a swim. When Faith heard about their plan she demanded to be taken along. She insisted they pick up Liana on the way.

They stopped at Liana's mother's house. She ran out the door and then slid into the back seat beside him. As they drove out to the canal, the wind lashed her hair around her face. She caught him looking at her as she reached up and tucked it inside the collar of her shirt.

They parked along the side of the road and then hiked down the levee to the diversion dam. While Faith spread a towel across the small, sandy beach, Wagner walked out onto the dam and stripped off his clothes. As he preened for Faith, who acted as if she was not at all amused, Liana walked out onto the dam behind him.

Without the slightest hesitation, she untied her bathing suit top and dropped it to the concrete. She glanced over to Cahill as she stepped out of her blue jeans and the suit bottom she wore underneath, and then with a single, sharp laugh she dove off the back of the dam, slicing through the surface of the pond backed up behind it. It was all he could do to breathe. He pulled his T-shirt over his head in such a hurry that he nearly tore off an ear, then peeled off his cutoffs and plunged in after her.

A week passed before he summoned the nerve to call her from the telephone booth behind the Mohawk station. He still remembered leaning back against the smudged glass walls, clutching the receiver in his sweating hands, waiting for her to answer. She told him her mother would never allow her to go to a movie with him—she wasn't quite fifteen—but she told him to meet her in front of the movie theater the next night. She said she'd tell her mother she was going to the movies with Faith. He remembered how the strategy came to her as easily as a dream.

He was there almost an hour early, pacing along the sidewalk until she and Faith arrived. After Faith left, they climbed up into the highest rows of the balcony, and there in the cool, elevated darkness they kissed and pawed each other. As the summer wore on they grew bolder and more desperate. He had no idea how many movies they saw. He couldn't remember any of them now.

Then one night late that summer she snuck out the window of her mother's house. He met her in the alley, and they drove the Mustang out to the back of the Johnson ranch. The moon had risen above the Sierra. In its pale light, he lifted her blouse. She arched her back and struggled out of her jeans, then she crossed her wrists over her eyes as if she couldn't bear to watch.

Afterward she wept in his arms. All the way back into town she lay across the seat with her head in his lap. Neither of them said a word.

Cahill hit on the cigarette again, then stubbed it out. He pushed up and crossed the room, and then he sat down beside her on the bed.

He could hear her breath passing softly through her lips. He carefully lifted her hair back off her face. He wondered if she was dreaming. He wondered if she was dreaming about Rosarito.

CHAPTER 11

"No!" HE SCREAMED.

He bolted up in bed as the sudden report of the .38 crashed off the bedroom walls. His face was drenched with sweat. His heart pounded in his chest. He was out of breath, as if he'd been running for miles.

But then he saw daylight, the hard blue sky through the balcony doors. He could hear the mourning doves cooing in the gardens below. He was still alive. She hadn't shot him. He hadn't screamed at all.

She was sleeping peacefully beside him, but she woke as he rolled off the bed, then knelt down before the nightstand.

"What are you doing?" she asked, suddenly alarmed.

Cahill slammed the bottom drawer, then stood up and started dressing. "I'm getting rid of the goddamn gun," he said.

He drove out to the Midway, then headed west. The air was sharp, the morning clear, washed by the storm. In the distance was Four Corners, the country market where St. Louis Road intersected the Midway. He'd turn south there and then take St. Louis Road down to the dredger ponds along Gossett Creek. He'd get rid of the .38 there.

He couldn't believe he'd dreamed she'd shot him. He closed his eyes for a second, took a deep breath. He couldn't clear it out of his mind.

As he approached the market he decided to stop for a cup of coffee. He lifted his foot from the accelerator and began to brake, but just as he started to pull up in front of the market he spotted Mooney's car in the parking lot. He jerked the wheel hard to the left and turned onto St. Louis Road, but he knew Mooney had seen him. As he sped away, he glanced up into the rearview mirror and could see Mooney hustling toward his car.

He didn't know what to do with the .38. He couldn't leave it in the glovebox, not on the chance Mooney might ask to see the Mustang's registration. But he had to do something with it, and he had to do it in a hurry. In the rearview mirror, Mooney was closing on him, lights flashing on the top of his car.

In desperation, he reached down and worked his fingers beneath the corner of the door panel. Years ago he'd removed it while installing speakers for a tape deck that had long since been stolen. He bent the panel back and slipped the .38 inside the door frame, then pounded the panel closed with his fist. It was the best he could do.

He guided the Mustang off the side of the road. As he came to a stop along the edge of a walnut orchard, he turned and looked back across the convertible top, folded down behind the back seat. Mooney had already climbed out of his car and was walking up to the Mustang. He was smiling broadly, as if they were old friends.

"Where are you headed in such a hurry?" he asked.

Cahill looked up at him. "What hurry?" he said.

"If I was a gambling man, I'd wager you just might have been out at the Harris ranch."

"I looked in on Liana this morning," Cahill admitted. "There's no crime in that, is there?"

"No, no," Mooney said. "It's damned Christian of you to look in on her first thing in the morning like this. You'd make Francis Robert proud."

Mooney glanced down at his watch, then looked up and smiled. "You surprise me, Winn. It's not even half past six. I'd have thought you were more the kind to stay up all night and sleep all day."

"I couldn't sleep," Cahill said.

Mooney wagged a finger at him. "That could be the sign of a guilty conscience," he said, but Cahill didn't say anything.

Mooney reached for his cigarettes. He tapped the pack against the heel of his hand, then unwrapped the cellophane.

"I was on my way to the Washout, Winn. You know we've been dragging that stretch of river for going on three days now and we still haven't found Tommy's body."

Mooney shook his head, then lit a cigarette and snapped his lighter shut. "It makes me wonder if maybe we're not gonna find the body—not there, anyways. You know what I mean? I mean maybe the body was never there in the first place."

Cahill stared up at him, a fire burning in the pit of his stomach.

Mooney squinted up at the sky, shading his eyes with his hand. "Well, these are the things I'm paid to wonder about," he said.

"So what do you want with me?" Cahill asked him. "Did I do something wrong?"

Mooney tugged at a nostril. "Actually, Winn, I did want to talk with you. I was meaning to drop by Francis Robert's this afternoon. I was hoping you'd explain to me why you lied about the Thunderbird Motel."

Cahill looked away into the maze of thick, white-painted trees. All he could think about was the .38 inside the car door.

"I'll tell you what, Winn. Why don't you get out of the car?" Mooney said.

"I took her back to Francis Robert's house," Cahill said.

"I said why don't you get out of the car, Winn."

Mooney reached down to the door handle; the hinges groaned as he pulled it open.

As Cahill climbed out, Mooney motioned for him to stand away from the Mustang.

"I didn't think it mattered," Cahill said. "I was afraid Faith might find out."

"Faith wouldn't much care for you bringing a woman back to Francis Robert's?"

"That's why I told you we went out to the Thunderbird."

Mooney smiled, the corner of his mouth turning up as if the confession brought him great satisfaction. Then he dragged on his cigarette.

"I knew you never took anyone out to the Thunderbird," he said. "I had myself a talk with Willis Allen yesterday. He's the manager there at the Thunderbird. You know Willis, don't you, Winn? He's a heavy-set boy, sits around all day and night watching television and drinking cream soda. Willis doesn't much care who stays in his motel or what they do there, so long as their checks don't bounce and they don't tear the rooms up so bad the maid can't clean up the mess."

Mooney laughed. "I don't mind telling you I gave old Willis religion. He must have thought I was going to haul that big ass of his down to the jailhouse, though I don't know for the life of me where he might have got himself an idea like that. Lord, he was sweating so bad his glasses kept sliding down his nose. He'd push them back up, but two seconds later they be right back down on the tip. I thought they were going to fall clean off his head."

Then Mooney shook his head, as if to chase the thought from his mind. "Well, Willis told me no Winn Cahill rented a room from him the other night, and I believed him, Winn. I knew Willis was telling me the truth. I get feelings about people, Winn—just like that," he said, snapping his fingers as loud as a clap of the hands. "I had a good feeling about Willis.

"But you know, Winn, I've got a bad feeling about you. I've had it ever since Liana told me about you and Tommy getting into it out at Hudson Grove."

"It was nothing," Cahill said. "Everybody there saw it was nothing. Tommy and Liana left. I went down to the Blue Orchid."

"And that's where you met this . . ." Mooney waited.

"Valentina," Cahill said.

"Her name was Valentina?"

"That's right."

"I'll bet you don't know her last name, do you?"

"I never asked."

"And you took her back to Francis Robert's, and no one else was there—no one actually saw you at the house because you didn't want anyone to know you were bringing this Valentina inside.''

"That's right," Cahill said.

Mooney pursed his lips. He whistled long and smooth. "Oh that's slick, isn't it. That's slicker than a preacher's prick in a calf's ass, Winn. And you want me to take your word on all this after you fed me that line of shit about the Thunderbird Motel?

"You see how this looks, don't you, Winn?''

Cahill didn't say anything as Mooney took another long drag on his cigarette.

"You know, Winn, I don't feel too good about Liana, either. I mean, you'd figure she'd be all shook up to hear Tommy might have drowned himself in the river, but she's as cool as cellar cider.''

"I don't see what any of that has to do with me," Cahill said.

Mooney smiled at him. "Give me time, Winn. I'm still working on this.''

Cahill pointed to the Mustang. "Do you mind if I get back in the car?'' he asked.

Mooney regarded him for a second, then shrugged as if it made no difference to him.

"You don't plan on leaving town anytime soon, do you, Winn? I'd like to think you were going to stick around until we get all this sorted out.''

"I'm not going anywhere," Cahill said as he slipped behind the wheel.

He reached out for the door, but Mooney

caught it and leaned down on it. "I'd hate to have to come after you, Winn. Do you understand what I'm saying? I mean to tell you I'm one lousy son of a bitch when I get crossed."

Then with both hands, Mooney slammed the door shut. The .38 banged loudly inside it.

"Sounds to me like you'd better get yourself another car, Winn. This old beater's falling apart."

The tires howled as he pulled up onto the grated steel span of the bridge over Gossett Creek. He glanced down at the creek. Between its densely wooded banks, the water flowed quietly toward its confluence with the Sacramento.

He braked, then turned down the narrow dirt road that tunneled along the opposite bank. Blackberries and wild grape formed a nearly impenetrable wall along both sides of the road. The low branches of the willows and elms brushed across the windshield. Waist-high Johnson grass grew between the deep set of ruts.

After half a mile, the road opened up onto a broad plain at the foot of the ridge of dredger tailings the mining companies had raked up from the creek bottom years ago. Cahill parked in the shade, then waited as the long roostertail of dust thrown up by the car drifted slowly across the clearing.

He waited a minute to be certain no one else

was there, then he reached down and pulled the door panel back and retrieved the .38. As he climbed out of the car and started down to the pond, he tucked it under his belt.

A turkey vulture circled high overhead, coasting on the thermals rising from the valley floor. Suddenly he heard a sharp rattle. He whirled around to his right, but it was only a lizard, darting into the brush from the bench of rock where it had been sunning itself.

At the edge of the brackish water he stood beside the hull of an upturned sedan, then took a last glance back up at the clearing. The valley was dead silent.

He hurled the .38 into the middle of the pond. It splashed quietly through the surface, and he stood there, glad to be rid of the gun, and watched the rings spread out toward the shore.

Then he looked up at the seamless sky and wondered when it all was going to end.

CHAPTER 12

In his one good suit, which meant he'd been to court that morning, Wagner was sitting on the porch at Francis Robert's house. In the mid-day heat, he had unbuttoned his shirt collar. His tie was pulled down, and his charcoal gray jacket was draped over the porch railing, as limp as a flag.

Cahill walked up to the house. He stood below the porch in the mottled shade of the camphor trees.

"Did you ever know Frank Hildalgo?" Wagner asked him.

Cahill didn't say anything.

"He used to work for the land company. He drove a bankout wagon during the harvest. He may also have worked during planting, but I can't remember for certain."

"Never heard of him," Cahill said.

"Not a bad kid, really," Wagner said, sipping at a bottle of soda. "He got himself into a little trouble some years back. I'm proud to say I was able to help him out of it."

"Is there a point to this, David Earle?"

"Hildalgo was charged with grand theft auto. Fortunately we were able to have the charges dismissed without prejudice after a conference with Art Goode, the deputy who arrested Hildalgo. This was after I was able to ascertain that in addition to the faithful discharge of his duties as an officer of the law, Goode had recently torched a boarding house he owned in order to collect the insurance settlement. So Goode and Hildalgo and I all sat down together, and everyone agreed to clean up their acts."

Wagner grinned, then leaned back and fanned himself with his hat. "Well, Goode and Hildalgo made such a pledge," he said. "It didn't seem necessary in my case.

"Anyway, Goode and I have kept in contact over the years. Periodically I solicit his opinion, and as a rule he's glad to work with me. Of course I go to him only on rare occasions, only when it's important. I wouldn't want to take advantage of our relationship."

Annoyed, Cahill walked up the steps, then pulled the screen door back and entered the house. Wagner followed him inside, through the living room and then into the kitchen, where Cahill drew a bottle of beer from the refrigerator.

"I talked to Goode this morning, Winn, while I was down at the courthouse. Do you know what he told me? Do you want to hear something truly insane?"

"What?"

"Goode says Mooney thinks you killed Tommy. He says Mooney thinks you and Tommy got into a fight over Liana. He thinks maybe that's how you picked up that gash on the back of your head. Mooney figures you dumped the truck in the river to cover it up. That's why there weren't any skid marks on the road. He thinks they haven't been able to turn up the body because the body was dumped somewhere else."

Cahill stared at him.

"In fact, Mooney called off the search this morning," Wagner said.

"He can't prove a thing," Cahill said.

"Mooney doesn't have to, Winn. That's not his job. That's for the district attorney. Mooney's job is to make arrests. That's what puts his picture in the newspaper. He'll arrest you. Then you'll go to arraignment. The D.A. will tell the judge you killed Calvin Gillespie's only son in cold fucking blood, and the judge will slap a bail on you that we'll never make. You could sit in jail for months before it ever comes to trial."

"I'm not sitting in jail," Cahill said, but Wagner wasn't listening to him.

"Let me tell you something else," Wagner said. "If Mooney thinks you killed Gillespie, then he's got to believe Liana saw it or heard it or at the very least knows how it went down. And if Mooney believes Liana's a witness, you can bet he and the D.A. are gonna go after her testimony.''

''And what's she going to say?'' Cahill snapped. ''What's she going to say without incriminating herself? She can take the Fifth.''

Wagner shook his head. ''That's not what I'm talking about.''

He reached up and rubbed his forehead. ''What if she decides to incriminate you, Winn?''

''What the hell are you talking about?''

''What if she puts the gun in your hands? What if she says you shot Tommy?''

''She won't,'' Cahill said.

''What if they make her an offer? What if fingering you is the only way she sees to keep her own ass out of the fire?''

''I said she won't!''

Wagner paused long enough to take a breath. ''I'm sorry, Winn, but I don't like it. I don't like any of this.''

''You're not supposed to like it, David Earle. You're supposed to handle it.''

''You want me to handle it? Then let me go down to the courthouse right now. Let me talk to Stanton Douglas.''

''No deal,'' Cahill said.

''Everybody deals, damn it. It's the law of the land.''

''I said no!''

''You want to play the hero for her, Winn? Is that it?''

"Get out of here, David Earle."

"What are you gonna do, Winn? What about tomorrow? What about the day after that? You think you're just going to walk away from this? You think it's all going to blow over? Well, you're wrong. You're dead wrong."

Cahill refused to listen. He turned and stared out the window above the sink. He didn't care if Wagner was right; he didn't care if it was the truth. The truth couldn't do him any good now.

"I'm telling you, Winn—you're the one who's gonna take the fall on this, and you can bet Liana knows it."

She came by that night. She knocked on the screen door, then pushed inside, a brown paper bag clutched to her chest.

"I had a craving for Chinese food," she said. "I couldn't help myself."

She crossed the living room and set the bag down on the table.

"Have you eaten?"

Cahill stared at her.

She stopped and looked at him. "Is something wrong?" she asked, but then she disappeared into the kitchen.

She came back and set two plates down on the table, then lifted the white takeout cartons from the bag.

"No forks," she said. "That's cheating."

She took a pair of wooden chopsticks out of their paper sleeve, broke them apart, then rubbed them together to remove any splinters. "These are half the fun.

"I went to the Imperial Palace," she said. "Do you know the Chinaman who runs the Imperial Palace? I don't think he's a Chinaman at all. He's got that long straight black hair and dark skin and that horrible goatee. He looks just like an Indian, if you ask me." She laughed at the thought. "What kind of Indian would try to pass himself off as a Chinaman?"

"That's enough!" Cahill shouted.

He slapped one of the cartons off the table, then grabbed another and threw it across the room. It exploded against the wall.

"Just listen to yourself!"

Stunned, she stood back out of his way, but that was all the damage he meant to do.

"Jesus," he sighed as he dropped back into the sofa.

She stared at him a moment, arms folded across her chest, coolly measuring his anger.

"I'll go get a mop and pail," she said.

She walked over to the door and gazed out through the screen. A cloud of moths swirled through the yellow light above the door, battering themselves against the hot bare bulb.

"You took the bandage off," she said.

He reached up to the rough stubble growing around the wound at the back of his head.

"Do you want me to take a look at it?"

"It'll be all right," he said.

She brushed her forehead with the back of a hand. "Did you get rid of the gun?"

He reached for his beer and took a swallow. "I got rid of it," he said.

"Where?"

"I threw it into the dredger ponds."

"Oh," she said, her voice sinking as if disappointed.

Then Cahill laughed.

"What's so funny?" she asked.

"I talked to David Earle this afternoon," he said. "He told me Mooney thinks I killed Tommy. Mooney thinks Tommy and I got into a fight over you."

She stared emptily at him.

"Mooney knows he's not going to find Tommy in the river. He's not even looking anymore."

"That doesn't make any sense," she said.

"Sure it does, Liana. It makes perfect sense."

Cahill allowed himself another laugh. "David Earle wants me to cut a deal with the district attorney. He wants me to go down to the courthouse and tell them what happened."

She stiffened.

"Don't worry, Liana. I told him no."

She brushed her hair back, then moved over to him. She knelt on the rug before the sofa, her hands on his knees.

"Maybe David Earle is right," she said softly. "Maybe I should go down and tell the sheriff what happened. Is that what you want? I'll do it if it is. I'll go down right now. I'll tell them the truth—that I shot Tommy, that I was afraid they wouldn't believe us, that I begged you to help me."

"It's too late, Liana. They'll never believe us now."

"I don't care," she said. "I'll do it anyway."

Cahill looked down at her. He needed to believe her; he needed to believe she'd do that for him. He needed the believing more than the truth itself.

He touched her cheek with his fingers, then pulled her up to him. They kissed long and deliberately until finally she broke away from him, like a swimmer exploding through the surface for air.

She slid down to the floor before him. She drew him out and then bowed over him. After a minute, she rode back onto her heels and shrugged her blouse off her shoulders. When she moved back to him, she took him in the swale between her breasts, clasping them together, enclosing him. The hard tremor of his loins arrived quickly. He was too tired to deny it.

He slumped back onto the sofa and watched her rub him into her skin.

Then she rested her head on the top of his knee. "I'll do anything for you, Winn Cahill. Anything you want."

* * *

Later that night, they lay on the old man's bed.

"I thought you would call this afternoon," she said. "I waited, but then when I knew you weren't coming I took Sonny for a ride. I rode out to the back of the ranch, then along the canal. There were kids fishing off the trestle. I chased them off," she said. "I told them it was private property."

"I wouldn't worry about it," he said.

But he did, and he knew she did too.

She must have thought he was asleep when she left. He watched her fumble through the dark for her clothes, and then he watched her go.

CHAPTER 13

HE WAS KILLING time by washing the Mustang when Faith pulled up in front of the house in her Falcon.

"Well, you'd better get a move on," she said. "David Earle called and told me to come tell you to meet him down at Cutter's."

"What does he want?"

"The son of a bitch wouldn't tell me, naturally. He just said for you to meet him there at eleven o'clock."

"What time is it now?"

"You've got ten minutes," she said.

"Jesus Christ."

He threw down the hose, slung the rag up onto the porch railing, then pushed into the house. Faith followed him down the hall to the bathroom. She stood outside the door while he urinated.

"He was up all night," she said. "He tossed and turned until I finally had to kick him out of the bed."

She moved into the doorway when she determined he was finished.

"Later I got up and found him in the living room, watching the television with the sound turned off."

"Maybe he's worried about the mailbox he ran over," Cahill said.

Faith stared at him for a second, then reached up and tucked a stray lock of hair behind her ear.

"Oh, he says he's got that all figured out. He says he's got some kid to come over and fix it as soon as he gets him out of jail. He's a rustler. Can you believe that? Who ever heard of anybody rustling cattle anymore? He told me the kid shot a steer up in Holmes Creek Canyon, dressed it out, then got arrested trying to sell the meat to the Johnson Steak House."

Faith shook her head disgustedly. "That's who David Earle says is going to fix the mailbox. The man collects losers."

Cahill dried his face, then draped the towel over his shoulder.

"Truth is, Winn, he's worried about you and Liana."

Cahill pushed past her, then picked his shirt off the back of the sofa and pulled it over his head.

"So what's he worried about me and Liana for?" he asked her.

Faith studied him a second. "He's heard the rumors, I'm sure."

"You don't believe that crap, do you?"

"It's bad, isn't it?"

Cahill crossed the street, then pushed in through the diner's heavy glass door. The air was burdened with the smell of grease and oil from the grill in the back. Long bars of light passed through the blinds in the windows and lay across the booths below. Taken by the owner of the diner, the head of a four-point buck was mounted on the wall above the counter, its antlers covered with dust, its eyes frozen in eternal astonishment.

Wagner was sitting in a booth in the back. Cahill walked past the glass bells covering plates of doughnuts and slices of pie, then slid into the booth across from him. Wagner looked up from a plate of fried eggs and griddle cakes dredged in syrup.

"You're late," he said.

"I see you found a way to kill the time," Cahill said.

Wagner glanced back down at the plate, then pushed it away. "There was a moment there in which I actually entertained the possibility of eating that," he said. "Fortunately I've come to my senses."

"Faith said you needed to see me," Cahill said.

Wagner leaned across the table, wrapping his hands around a glass of iced tea. "I thought you might like to know Mooney found your Valentina,'' he said.

Cahill stared emptily at him. ''What are you talking about?'' he asked in a voice that barely reached a whisper.

''Her name isn't Valentina at all,'' Wagner said. ''Her name is Louise. She's married to an Indian named Eddie Logan.''

Wagner leaned back, extending his arm along the top of the seat. His fingers tugged at the padding that escaped through a torn seam in the Naugahyde.

''Are Goode called me this morning,'' he said. ''He told me Logan was out of town for a couple days. When he got back, he got the idea that this Louise might have been running around on him while he was gone. She denied it, of course. She admits she went down to the Blue Orchid once or twice. She admits she closed it down a couple nights. She even admits that one night she left to get a room at the Thunderbird with some guy. But she swears it was all a joke. She tells Logan she drove straight home.''

Wagner laughed. ''I don't guess you could blame Logan for not believing a word of it. So he puts away a half a bottle of scotch, then gets out his deer rifle and starts shooting the place up.

''Goode was the first deputy to respond. He managed to talk Logan into laying the rifle down, and then he arrested the dumb bastard and hauled him in.''

Wagner reached out and drained the glass of iced tea, never taking his eyes off Cahill.

''Goode figured that was pretty much the end of it. He figured Stanton Douglas might ring him up on some petty firearm beef, but he knew they'd bargain it all down. Hey, Logan thought his wife was cheating on him. He had a right to go a little crazy.

''Well, this morning Mooney happened to see Goode's report. Goode says the minute he saw that bit about the Blue Orchid and the Thunderbird, his eyes lit up and he was gone.''

''Jesus,'' Cahill sighed. He closed his eyes. His head was filled with a terrible noise, like the beating of thousands of wings. He could feel it all crashing down around him.

Wagner raised the glass again and took a piece of ice in his mouth. He sucked on it a second, then spat it back into the glass.

''You're in deep shit here, Winn.''

Cahill looked up.

''When Mooney finds out your story's no good he's going to come down on you with both feet.''

Cahill reached across the booth to the stainless steel napkin holder. He pinched several napkins and pulled them out and wiped his mouth. ''So what do I do now?'' he asked.

''It's over, Winn. It's time for you and me to

walk down to the courthouse and get all this straightened out.''

''No,'' he said.

''You don't have any choice,'' Wagner said, frustration rising in his voice.

''I said no.''

''What do you mean, no?'' Wagner snapped as Cahill slid out of the booth and started for the door.

''Where the fuck are you going?'' Wagner shouted after him.

He came up on the harvester in a hurry. Traveling no more than twenty-five miles an hour, it was heading west on the Midway, straddling the broken white line painted down the center of the road, blocking both narrow lanes. A young Mexican rode high in the harvester's green cab, radio headphones clamped down over his ears.

Cahill hit the horn to get his attention, but the Mexican didn't hear him. He hit the horn a second time; he held it down—still to no avail.

There was no way to pass on the left side of the road, so he ducked over to the right, toward the edge of the asphalt. The shoulder was tight and then rose sharply up the back of an irrigation ditch, but he couldn't wait. There was no telling how much time they had. For all he knew Mooney had already obtained a warrant for his arrest.

He let the Mustang creep further to the right,

off the pavement. As the tires dug into the soft gravel, the car pulled hard to the right, but he held the wheel straight and then stomped on the accelerator. The car surged forward, then shot past the harvester in the shadow of its huge knobbed tires and then swerved back onto the roadway.

He raced out to the ranch, then turned in through the gate and followed the palms up to the house. Before the engine completely died, he was running up to the front door. As he stormed through, it swung back and crashed against the wall. Pulling himself up by the bannister, he took the stairs to Liana's bedroom three at a time, then burst through the door.

She was standing across the room, her back against the wall. The instant she saw it was Cahill, she sank into the wicker chair beside the vanity.

"Christ, you scared me!"

"We're taking off," he said.

"What are you talking about?"

He crossed the room to her closet, then reached up and grabbed a leather suitcase and tossed it onto the bed. "We're leaving—now."

"To go where?" she demanded.

"Mexico."

She laughed at him, her mouth tight. "What are you talking about?"

"I said move!"

"We can't go to Mexico."

"The hell we can't!"

"It doesn't make sense. Not now. Not yet."

"It makes a hell of a lot more sense than sitting around waiting for Mooney to throw my ass in jail."

He pulled out the top drawer of her bureau and dumped the clothes into the suitcase, then he hurled the drawer out onto the balcony, where it banged against the railing.

"Mexico was your idea," he said. "Or don't you remember? This was all your idea!"

She rushed up to him and grabbed both his wrists. "Listen to me," she said. "You go ahead. You go now. Give me a week, two weeks at the most. Then I'll come down. I'll stay until I can sell the ranch, then I'll meet you in Rosarito."

She tugged hard on his arms. "I have to stay here, don't you see? We can't live in Mexico without money."

He couldn't believe it. She was cutting him loose again, just as she had when he first left for L.A. He tore away from her. Wagner was right. He was going to take the fall for her, and she was going to watch him go down.

She came after him again. She wrapped her arms around his waist. In a rage, he twisted away from her and drew back his arm, his hand clenched into a fist, but then he couldn't do it.

He shoved her away. She collapsed to the floor, crashing back into the nightstand. The lamp toppled to the floor and shattered beside her. He grabbed her handbag and emptied it onto the bed, then he tore her wallet open and rifled through it.

"Take it!" she screamed. "Take it all!"

He turned back to her as he shoved the thin wad of bills into his pocket.

She ran out the front door after him. In the middle of the courtyard, she sank to her knees. The sun angled down around her through the overgrown gardens. The air was filled with the furious sizzling of insects and the fragile, frightened melodies of the songbirds.

The Mustang's tires bit into the gravel drive. As he raced back out to the Midway, he wondered if she'd known all along that he'd be the one to run.

CHAPTER 14

WHEN HE FIRST noticed the light blue smoke trailing the Mustang, he thought it was merely a film on the rearview mirror. Then he discovered he couldn't rub it off the glass. He glanced down at the dashboard and saw the engine was running hot. When he pressed down on the accelerator, he couldn't mistake the sudden loss of power.

He turned off the highway and found a gas station near the port in Sacramento. He raised the hood. The dipstick was too hot to remove without a rag. The minute he saw that the tip of the stick was dry, he knew he was in trouble.

He walked up to the office and bought four quarts of oil from the owner, a thick square-headed man whose face was covered with liver spots. As he returned to the car, the owner followed him out of the office, then began filling the tank with gas.

Cahill stabbed a pouring spout into the top of the first can of oil and turned it into the engine, then he tossed the rag over the radiator cap and carefully released it. A cloud of hissing steam boiled out. He waved the steam out of his face, then guided the water hose into the radiator.

"There's water leaking into one of the cylinders," the owner said as he leaned back against the pump. "I seen that right as you pulled in. I seen the steam in the exhaust. I'd bet good money the head gasket's cracked."

Cahill tried to ignore him. Even if the diagnosis was right, there was nothing he could do about it now.

"How far you going?" the owner asked him.

Cahill poured the second can of oil into the engine, but then he began to worry the owner might misunderstand his silence.

"L.A.," he said.

The owner laughed through his nose, then dragged his oil-blackened fingernails through the coarse gray stubble beneath his chin.

"You'll never make it, son."

"I'll make it," Cahill said.

It took all afternoon and evening to drive down the valley, stopping every twenty or thirty miles or so to pour another quart of oil into the engine and fill the radiator back up with water.

Outside Bakersfield he pulled into a truck stop. The dessicated foothills of the Coast Range had already folded into shadow. The sun had dropped behind them. Dozens of diesel rigs were lined up across the plain of asphalt that surrounded the cinder-block diner. The high, chromed sleeper cabs gleamed in the floodlights that ringed the lot.

Cahill parked behind the diner, out of view of the highway, then pushed in through the glass door. In the booths along the front window, truckers hunched over their books, cribbing the miles they'd traveled and the time it had taken them. His heart skipped as the flat, nasal voice of a highway patrol dispatcher came over the radio above the stainless steel window to the kitchen, advising that a woman had abandoned her car along the highway and had been reported walking south along the shoulder. A bawdy chorus of truckers volunteered to pick her up, but none moved toward the door.

He found a seat at the counter, which enabled him to sit with his back to the booths along the window. A young waitress with her dark hair pulled back in a bun filled his cup with coffee. Her eyes were plaintive and forlorn; her smile was split by a dark gap between her two front teeth. He ordered potatoes and eggs and ate them slowly.

He wondered if the warrant had been issued for his arrest yet. Mooney had surely made his way out to the Harris ranch by now. He wondered what Liana had told him—how long it would be before she told Mooney that he had killed Tommy. Maybe she already had. Now that he was gone, it would be a simple act of self-defense. His taking off would only confirm what Mooney already believed.

He wiped the plate with a piece of bread until it shone like it had just been washed, then slipped three dollars under the edge of his plate and walked outside. As he crossed the parking lot shards of broken glass popped beneath his boots. The steady, sonorous clattering of the diesel engines filled the night, and he could smell the sweet exhaust.

He slipped behind the wheel of the car. The engine turned over easily but didn't catch. He paused and waited a minute, then tried again. Still it wouldn't start. As the battery ran down, his own strength seemed to drain away with it. He tried again. Then it wouldn't turn over at all.

He slumped forward, resting his forehead on the steering wheel. Without lifting his head, he tried the key once more. It produced only a weak click.

A scream rose in his throat. He pushed back in the seat and furiously pumped the accelerator pedal. Closing his eyes, he reached for the key a final time, praying for a miracle, a single, divine spark, but there was nothing.

He threw his shoulder against the door and got out of the car. As he stared down into the dark engine, he could smell the gasoline flooding down the walls of the carburetor.

Then the back door to the kitchen swung open. Dragging a plastic barrel of garbage, a teenage boy in a white dishwasher's apron backed across the pavement toward a dark green dumpster bin.

Cahill quickly stepped up to help him. Together they hoisted the barrel up and emptied it into the bin.

The boy stared at Cahill. In the light pouring out the door his skin looked pale and sickly, but his shoulders were grown over with sinewy cords of muscle.

"I could have done it myself," he said quietly.

"I need a push," Cahill said, pointing at the Mustang.

The boy glanced into the kitchen, then reluctantly followed him across the pavement. Cahill reached in and took the car out of gear, and they began pushing it across the asphalt, Cahill straining against the side of the windshield, the boy in back, both hands flattened on the trunk.

When they got it rolling, Cahill swung in behind the wheel, jammed it into second, then dropped the clutch. The tires barked on the pavement. The Mustang bucked and caught and then abruptly pulled away from the boy; he spilled hard onto his shoulder and hip.

Cahill gunned the engine to keep it from dying. A cloud of smoke churned up behind the car. He turned and looked back over the folded top. Through the smoke, he could see the boy limping back toward the diner, rubbing his arm as if trying to regain the feeling in it. There wasn't time to see if he was all right.

He returned to the highway, relieved to be back on the road, but almost immediately the engine began to knock. With each mile the sound grew louder and retreated deeper into the block. A knot formed in his stomach. Squinting into the shallow field of light thrown by the headlights, he was afraid to go any faster than fifty miles an hour.

Then he took on the Grapevine, the long, winding stretch of highway that rose up out of the valley and then descended back down into the Los Angeles basin. The steep grade forced him to downshift into second, then into first. He crept over to the far right lane, where the southbound diesels ran up onto his rear bumper and blasted him with their air horns, then angrily pulled out to pass him. Twice they nearly ran him onto the shoulder. His grip on the steering wheel tightened. His knuckles were white as bone.

He began singing to himself, talking to the Mustang. He congratulated the car for each mile it delivered; he begged it to keep going. He rocked back and forth in his seat, as if to give the engine a lift. He rubbed the dashboard as if to assuage its pain.

He had to get to L.A. He had no idea where else to go. He didn't know what he was doing, only that he'd have to ditch the Mustang as soon as he got there. As soon as Mooney was issued the warrant for his arrest, they'd be looking for the car. They were probably looking for it now. Mooney would know he was likely headed south; he would have alerted the highway patrol.

He felt like he was driving into his own grave.

CHAPTER 15

STEELE LIVED IN Santa Monica with an actress named Yolanda Klein. It was almost three in the morning when Cahill pulled into the alley that ran behind the house she had inherited from her mother, then nosed the Mustang up to a row of dented garbage cans. One of the metal lids slid off and banged on the ground. A cat quickly clawed over the fence and then was gone.

He crossed the backyard, then tried the door to the service porch. It was locked, so he knocked sharply, then stepped back down from the door and looked up at the bedroom window upstairs. There was no response. After a minute he pounded on the door with his fist.

Finally a light came on in the bedroom. Heavy footsteps descended the stairs.

"Who the fuck is it?" Steele growled through the door.

"It's me," Cahill said.

He reached up to the screen door handle. Suddenly it crashed back into him, knocking him down the steps. Steele burst through it. Before Cahill could push back up, Steele was on him, grabbing a fistful of his hair and driving his face into the grass.

"You son of a bitch," Steele hissed, his mouth at Cahill's ear as if he meant to bite it off. "I've been waiting for this."

But Cahill arched his back and lifted himself up; he threw an elbow that caught Steele at the base of the neck and then he scrambled out from beneath him.

Steele made no move to come after him. Down on a knee, he stared at his bloodied hands. "Jesus Christ," he said quietly.

Cahill staggered over to the steps and sat down hard. He could feel the blood running down the back of his neck. He reached up and could feel the loose flap of skin, his wounded scalp torn open again.

Then the screen door opened behind him. In a long red bathrobe, Yolanda leaned against the frame. She took a drag on her cigarette, then exhaled into the night.

"Maybe you boys ought to continue this discussion inside," she said.

Then she turned and retreated into the house. Neither of them moved until she turned on the light in the kitchen. Then Steele rose slowly to his feet.

"Go on," he said. "The bitch is right."

* * *

Cahill went inside, into the service porch, then made his way into the kitchen. Yolanda was sitting at the table with a nearly empty bottle of champagne. In a cheap drugstore frame, a publicity still from a B-grade western in which she'd starred as the madame of a Mexican brothel hung on the wall above her. She had dark eyes and long black hair and a strong, aquiline nose. Her name was looped exuberantly across the lower righthand corner of the publicity still.

As Cahill sat down across from her, Steele tossed him a towel. He pressed it against the back of his head to staunch the bleeding while Steele washed his hands in the sink.

"Are you all right?" she asked him, though it was clear she had already concluded he was.

"Yeah," he said.

She tugged the cork out of the champagne bottle, then poured herself a glass. A few isolated bubbles rose from the bottom of the glass, then the surface was as still as a pond.

"We don't often get visitors this time of night," she said, watching him as she took a sip.

"I was in the neighborhood," Cahill said. "I thought I'd stop by and say hello."

"No shit?"

Cahill lowered the towel and examined the blood that soaked it.

"Winn and I have a little business to talk about," Steele said to Yolanda. "You understand what I'm saying?"

She looked out the window. The moon fought through the gritty air, a hazy, undefined globe.

"Yes, I believe I can understand that," she said. "I understand that whenever men want to be left alone, they say they've got business to talk about—which usually means they want to talk about women."

As she rose from the table, her robe briefly fell open and revealed a flash of dark thigh. She noticed it and smiled and didn't trouble to cover herself.

"You take care of yourself, Winn. You never were one who could afford many blows to the head."

"I'll try to remember that with what's left of my mind," he said.

Steele sat down in the chair vacated by Yolanda. He wrapped his hands around the base of the empty champagne bottle.

"We're through," he said. "They fired us that night."

Cahill knew better than to say anything.

"It was a good gig," Steele said, his voice rising. "It was steady work. It was easy fucking money."

"I know," Cahill said, but Steele ignored him.

"So what the hell are you doing here?"

Cahill took a deep breath. "I'm in a jam," he said.

"You're breaking my heart."

"I need money."

Steele stared at him a minute, then rocked back in his chair. He laughed as if appreciating some raunchy joke, arms folded across his chest.

"You want *me* to give *you* money?" Steele asked, pointing first at Cahill, then drilling himself in the chest with an index finger.

"You've got my Stratocaster. You've got my amp. You can hawk them both. I don't care."

"Why me? Why in the middle of the god-damn night? What did you do?"

He didn't know what to say; he wasn't sure how much to confess. "I went home," he said. "I ran into Liana. We got in a little trouble."

"What trouble?"

Cahill shrugged. "She shot a guy."

Steele laughed nervously, involuntarily. "She killed him?"

Cahill nodded reluctantly.

"So what are you doing here? Where's she?"

Cahill took a deep breath, then let it out slowly. "They think I did it," he said. "I'm trying to get down to Baja to let all this cool out."

Steele laughed again—louder this time. "That's priceless, Winn. You ought to sell this shit to the comics."

Cahill stared at him.

"What about her?"

"She's gonna come down later—she's gonna meet me in Rosarito after she sells her ranch."

Steele stood up. "Let me get this straight," he said. "Liana wastes some poor bastard, only everyone thinks you did it. So you oblige them all by taking off for Mexico, and Liana, sweetheart that she is, promises to sell the ranch and then come down later with the money. Is that about right?"

Cahill stared emptily at him. Suddenly he felt exhausted, defeated.

Steele leaned down into Cahill's face, flattening his palms on the table. "And you honestly think she's going to show up?" Steele pushed himself back up. "Sure she is, Winn. Sure she is."

He started toward the door to the stairs. "I'll hawk the Stratocaster for you. I'll sell your amp." He turned back to Cahill. "Where do I send the money?"

"The beach hotel—in Rosarito."

Steele nodded. "Now get the fuck out of here," he said.

As he walked around the front of the Mustang, he could feel the heat seeping out from beneath the hood. The smell of burnt oil rode in the air.

He slipped behind the wheel and pressed the gas pedal to the floor; he took a quick breath, then gave the key a quick turn of the wrist. Unexpectedly, the engine fired. He pumped the accelerator hard, revving it up to keep it from dying, the rods and wrist pins knocking inside the block as if the pistons might explode through the hood. Before it idled back down, he dropped it into gear and took off down the alley.

He drove across the city, then headed toward the beach. Near the boardwalk in Venice he found a closed-down Chinese restaurant called the Golden Dragon. Vulgar epithets had been spray-painted across the sheets of plywood nailed up over the windows. A For Sale sign was nailed to the gilded, hand-carved door. The time had come to lose the Mustang. He turned into the parking lot and killed the engine, then he hustled away from the car before anyone noticed him.

He made his way into the Canal District. In the distance a woman screamed. The sound froze him for a second. He waited until he heard her delirious laughter, then he pitched the Mustang's keys into the water and hurried across the bridge.

There was a light on in Darlene's kitchen. Her sister Marilyn was sitting at the table. A sleeveless T-shirt hung loosely from her cream-colored shoulders. Her long, fiery red hair was pulled up into a ponytail at the top of her head with a purple ribbon. She leaned forward and stabbed a fork into a saucepan on the table in front of her, then lifted a huge clump of macaroni and cheese up to her mouth.

He rapped once on the door. She swallowed, then dropped the fork into the saucepan as he let himself inside.

"Hello, Marilyn," he said.

She rose from the table and crossed the kitchen to the sink. "You're a day late, cowboy."

He didn't say anything.

"I suppose it would have killed you to make a phone call?"

"What are you talking about?"

"She called in sick just so she could wait around by the telephone all night. I warned her against it, but she just knew you were going to give her a call."

Cahill stared at her.

"I'm talking about the simple things, cowboy. Like remembering a girl's birthday, for one."

"Jesus," he said. "I didn't know."

"You mean you blew it off. And now you're going to stomp into her bedroom and wake her up, now that she's finally got herself asleep?"

She shook her head reproachfully. She was nearly six feet tall, with green eyes and eyelashes that waved like wings.

"What happened to your head, cowboy? You finally get what you deserved?"

He reached up to the back of his head. The bleeding had stopped, but his hair was as stiff as the bristles of a push broom.

"I have no idea what the girl sees in you."

* * *

Quietly he opened the bedroom door. In the light of the streetlamp filtering in through the curtains, he crossed the room to her bed. She was sleeping facing the wall. Above her, stenciled onto a pink tapestry with a tasseled fringe, was Elvis's grotesquely innocent face.

Cahill knelt down beside the bed and leaned over her. Her breath was warm, as sweet as milk. He began mouthing "Happy Birthday" into her ear, his voice barely louder than a whisper. After a second, a smile spread over her face. He stopped and kissed her cheek.

"Keep going," she said, her eyes still closed. "Sing it all the way through."

When he was finished, she pulled him down to her and kissed him. "I knew you'd come," she said.

"I missed your birthday," he said. "I know it was yesterday."

"But you were gone. You couldn't help it," she said, apologizing for him. "When did you get back?"

"Just now," he said. "I had some car trouble."

"See? See what I mean? You had good reason."

He stroked the side of her face, brushing back her long brown hair. "I should have given you a call."

"It's no big deal," she said.

"We could have done something."

"What?" she asked him, excited to indulge herself with the possibilities. "What would we have done?"

"I don't know," he said. "Maybe we would have gone out to dinner, someplace special, someplace expensive."

She slipped her arms around his neck. "I know what you can do for me," she said. "You can do it for me right now."

She wanted him behind her. On her hands and knees, she reached back between her legs and guided him into her. She took him almost reluctantly, with a sweetly pained cry. He was exhausted. He felt only relief when she cried out and fell away from him. As she sprawled before him on the mattress, he had to reach out to the wall to steady himself, to keep from toppling onto the floor.

"Lean back," she said to him.

He stretched out across the mattress. She knelt beside him and then delivered him with her hands.

As she stretched out alongside him, she seemed to have gained new energy. He could barely keep his eyes open; he could hardly hear her.

She got up and disappeared into the bathroom. For a moment he slipped into sleep. He woke with a start as she sank back down to the mattress, the perfume she'd found in the bathroom washing over him, as strong and heady as gasoline fumes.

"What's that?" he asked.

"It's Marilyn's. You don't like it?"

"How much did you put on?"

"Don't worry," she said. "She'll never miss it." She sniffed her wrists. "It's called Tabu," she said. "I think it's expensive." She draped an arm across his chest. "What's wrong, cowboy?"

"I'm just tired," he said.

"Did you see her?"

He closed his eyes and could see Liana running out the door of the house, then sinking to her knees in the courtyard. He couldn't believe how close he'd come to hitting her, how much he hated her. Steele was right. She was never going to meet him in Baja.

He took a deep breath. "It was a mistake," he said. "It was all a mistake."

She squeezed him, then rested her head on his shoulder. "I'm just glad you're back," she said.

He looked up at the shadows moving across the ceiling. The curtains sighed in the breeze moving in off the ocean. Soon it would be getting light.

He knew he was taking advantage of her, but she was the only one he could think of who'd help him across the border. She'd do anything for him, anything he asked, and he was desperate—for her car, for a few hours of sleep in the sanctuary of her house.

"How would you like to drive down to Tijuana tomorrow?"

She pushed up off the mattress. "For my birthday?" she exclaimed.

"Why not?" he said.

CHAPTER 16

ALREADY DRESSED, DARLENE stood in the bedroom window, balancing anxiously on her left leg. At the pockets and along the seams, her blue jeans were faded nearly to white. She wore a loose white peasant blouse and blue canvas deck shoes.

She turned to Cahill as he entered the room behind her. He tossed his towel onto the bed, then pulled on his pants. She watched him suck in his stomach to button them up.

"You never told me what you did to your head," she said.

Cahill carefully pushed his head through the neck of his black T-shirt. He winced as it tugged at the wound in his scalp, then sat down on the edge of the bed and stomped his feet into his boots.

"Does it hurt?"

He looked up at her. She saw he didn't want to talk about it.

"I don't have any money," she said, advancing her poverty cautiously. "Well, I've got six dollars. That's all."

"Don't worry about it. I've got money enough for the both of us."

"What about Marilyn?"

"What about her?"

Darlene walked over to the mirror on the back of the closet door. She curled her hair around a finger.

"She wants to go."

"I don't care," he said. "She can come as long as she's ready to go right now."

"She likes to drive."

"Forget it," he said.

She looked back over her shoulder at him. "I told her it was all right."

"It's not all right," he said.

He rose from the bed and crossed the room to pick up his duffel bag, on the floor in front of the closet door. She stepped aside, out of his way.

"You seem all jumpy," she said.

It was almost two o'clock before they gassed up the Rambler and got on the San Diego Freeway. Darlene sat beside him; in the back seat Marilyn leaned disconsolately against the door.

A hot wind had picked up, whipping sheets of newspaper across the sky. The air smelled like burning plywood. Tall, glassy office buildings rose on both sides of the highway, their mirrored surfaces reflecting the weary palms that grew among them. Traffic was thick. He was sweating freely as they crawled down the highway.

As soon as the traffic opened up, he pulled off the highway and found a liquor store and bought a quart of beer. He drank it as they drove down to San Diego.

Darlene and Marilyn had gotten into a fight while he was in the liquor store, and for the moment, at least, they were coolly ignoring each other. He didn't care what their quarrel was about. He was grateful for the silence.

Then traffic stopped.

"Now what?" Marilyn complained.

Darlene cast her a sidelong glance. A flatbed truck had rolled onto its side, spilling a load of furniture onto the pavement, blocking all the lanes. The driver and his teenage son were scrambling across the highway, dragging the broken furniture off to the shoulder.

"If you're in such an all-fired hurry, why don't you get out and help," Darlene said to her.

"Fuck you," Marilyn said.

Finally a single lane was cleared. Traffic converged on it. As they waited to merge into the open lane, a red Corvette swept by on the highway shoulder, throwing up a long plume of dust. The driver was young and tan and strikingly handsome. In the seat beside him, a blond woman shrieked through blood-red lips.

The Corvette tried to cut back into traffic in

front of the Rambler. Cahill sped up to block them out, then hit the horn, but it produced no sound. Infuriated he pounded it with his fist. Still it didn't work.

Darlene looked on helplessly. "It's broken," she said.

"Nothing works on this old piece of shit anymore," Marilyn said.

"Which is precisely why I'm going to sell it," Darlene said. "Then I'm going to buy me something new, like a sports car."

"With what?" Marilyn asked, turning to look at her.

"When I sell the Rambler, then I'll have the money," Darlene said.

Marilyn laughed at her. "Who's going to be dumb enough to buy this old heap?"

Darlene turned to Cahill. "I'll sell it," she said. "Ronnie turned the mileage back. One day he disconnected the speedometer cable, and then he turned the mileage back with his electric drill."

"Then the son of a bitch ran out on you."

Darlene spun around to her.

Marilyn laughed, then looked out the window. "He was some kind of husband, all right."

"That's enough!" Cahill shouted. "Shut the fuck up, both of you!"

They were almost there. Traffic had slowed again, thickening at the border. Darlene and Marilyn shrank back into their seats. Neither of them said a word as he pulled in behind an old Volkswagen bus. Its battered, light green body was smeared with bumper stickers from across the country. An American flag fluttered from the radio antenna.

As they inched toward the huge blue arch that marked the border, his nerves began working on him. The beer had soured in his stomach. Sweat streamed down his brow.

He pursed his lips and let out his breath, then wiped the perspiration from around his mouth. Ahead, the van abruptly lurched through the gate and across the border.

Cahill pulled the Rambler up beside the booth between the lanes. A young guard immediately stepped out from behind it. His smooth face gave away nothing. In his dark, neatly pressed uniform, he looked like a soldier, rigid and obedient and slightly frightened, yet filled with a sense of his own power and authority.

The guard scanned the Rambler quickly, checking the license plate, then squinting through the windshield as if he might recognize them. Cahill swallowed hard, smothering the urge to throw open the door and run for his life. His jaw ached from grinding his teeth.

Then without so much as a word, the guard waved them through, across the border into Mexico.

They found a room in Tijuana. The motel was run by a hunchbacked old woman in a long black dress. Beneath her shawl, her steely gray hair was as coarse as straw. Her dark skin bagged beneath her piercing eyes and kinked black hairs grew out of the tip of her chin.

Strings of colored Christmas lights had been put up around the office window. On the wall behind the desk, crucified in a gilded wooden frame, Christ watched over the old woman. Cahill tried to barter the price of the room down, but she wouldn't budge from eight dollars. As he peeled off the bills, she eyed him suspiciously.

He emerged from the office, then motioned for Darlene to drive the car down to the far end of the courtyard. The three single-story wings of the motel enclosed an empty fountain. Tall blades of grass grew up through cracks in the bottom of the dry reflecting pool. Sustained by a slow leak, slick orange moss bled down the side of the fountain.

Room nineteen was hot and cramped. Thick velvety curtains doused the late afternoon sun. Cahill had to duck to avoid the light bulb screwed into a porcelain socket in the ceiling. Darlene and Marilyn filed into the room after him.

He closed the door, then turned on the small electric fan and dropped into a frayed cane chair pushed up against the wall.

Marilyn promptly began rifling through the drawers of the bureau. She produced a tattered

Bible, fanned through the pages with her thumb, then dropped it beside the television.

"Why doesn't anybody ever leave anything good?" she wanted to know.

At the foot of the bed Darlene stared down at the mattress covered with a white, black and brown Aztecan wool blanket.

"We're supposed to sleep on that?"

"I'm starving," Marilyn said. "I want something to eat."

"We'll wait until after dark," Cahill said.

"You think I came down here to kill time in this dump?" Marilyn snapped. "I want to go to the dog races."

"What the fuck do you care about the dog races?" Cahill said as she walked into the bathroom.

Without troubling to close the door, she hiked up her blue dress and sat down on the toilet, her knees knocked together, ankles splayed apart.

Cahill pushed up out of the chair and then sat on the bed so he didn't have to look at her. He stretched out and leaned back against the wooden headboard. Darlene clicked on the television, then sat down beside him. Broadcast over the border, a game show appeared through a field pf primitive light. The studio audience screamed.

"Do you feel all right?" Darlene asked him. "You look like you've got a fever."

Cahill ignored her as Marilyn walked out of the bathroom.

"There was a poster I saw that said the dog races start at eight o'clock. I'm going," she announced.

Darlene ran her hand over Cahill's face, but he pushed it away. She stood up immediately, dark crescents of perspiration soaking through her blouse beneath each breast.

"I'm going with you," she said to Marilyn. "The cowboy can lie in bed all night for all I care."

Cahill closed his eyes. He reached up to the bridge of his nose. His skin was gritty with salt. He'd thought he'd feel relieved when he crossed the border into Mexico. He thought he'd feel free, released. Instead he could feel it all unraveling on him, and there was nothing he could do to stop it.

Two minutes later, Darlene walked back into the room and dropped into the cane chair.

"It didn't seem right, leaving you here," she said.

She rose and stood in front of the fan and lifted her blouse away from her stomach so the air could blow up under it.

"What do I want to watch some dogs running around the track for? They're so skinny, like they've been starved. They don't look like any dog I'd ever have."

"What about Marilyn?"

She shrugged and turned back to him. "She'll be back later."

Darlene slipped a finger through Cahill's belt and followed him past the shabby storefronts and the stunted palms blackened with soot and exhaust. Children tugged at their pantlegs, pulling them toward unlit alleys. Strung above the street, a sagging canopy of electrical wires sparked and snapped as if at any minute it might all collapse and burst into fire.

"I want you to buy me a present," she said.

Cahill looked at her.

"What kind of birthday is it without a present from your guy?" she asked him.

They were standing in front of a liquor store. "Wait here," he said.

She leaned back against the wall while he stepped inside and bought a bottle of mescal. She squealed with delight when he handed it to her. Without wasting a second, she twisted off the cap and took a long swallow, then she handed it to him. He took a drink too, and as they continued down the street she slipped her hand into his.

They came to a small, wooden taco stand set up amid the rubble of an unfinished cinder-block building. Its corrugated tin roof deflected the light of the streetlamp at the corner. A heavy-set girl with long black hair stared out from the shadows below. She smiled as they walked up to her.

On a chalkboard, the prices of the tacos were listed in a careless hand, as if they might rise or fall on a whim. Shrimp and squid and pig's feet swam in large glass jars that lined the counter. Dark red strips of meat hung from a string behind the dark-haired girl.

Cahill couldn't even remember the last time he'd eaten. He pointed at the meat. "What's that?"

"*Pierna,*" she said through a row of teeth as tiny and sharp as a handsaw blade.

"I don't understand."

She shrugged and looked past him. "*Pierna,*" she said. "It is leg."

"Leg of what?" he pressed.

She shrugged. "Leg," she said.

He gave up easily. "All right," he said. "Give me one of those."

"I want one too," Darlene said, and the girl nodded agreeably.

He watched her heat the corn tortilla over a ring of blue flames produced by a camp stove, then fill it with beans and strips of the grilled *pierna* dredged through a tin of red sauce. She handed it to him. Wrapped in foil, it was so hot he could barely hold it. He took a bite. Flames seemed to rush through his nose. His eyes burned; sweat beaded up across his forehead.

"Goat," Darlene said. "I'll bet it's goat."

Cahill sat in the cane chair. In her panties, Darlene stood before him and filled his glass again.

The mescal lent a hallucinogenic blue shadow to everything he saw.

"That's enough," he said. As he pulled the glass away, mescal poured out the mouth of the bottle and splashed onto the slab floor.

"Look what you've done now," she playfully scolded him.

"Sorry," he said.

He watched her move over to the window, where she had arranged two other glasses. She filled one glass, carefully raised the level to the lip, then moved on to the next. When they were both filled, she raised the bottle and studied the worm lying on the bottom. Two fingers of mescal remained. She studied the bottle a minute. Then she laughed and poured the rest of the mescal into her open hand. It spilled through her fingers and then onto the floor until finally the worm lay in her palm.

Cahill winced as she dropped the bottle to the floor, but it didn't break and rolled instead beneath the bed.

"Are you ready, cowboy?" she asked.

"It's all yours," he said.

She took a deep breath, then licked the worm out of her hand. Eyes wide, she swallowed hard. She grimaced; her body shook. Then she burst out laughing.

"I did it!" she exalted as she staggered across the room and fell on the bed.

"Congratulations."

She beamed, then struggled up to stand. She

slapped her hands on her hips, then dipped her chin below her shoulder and peered down at him. "I'm all yours," she said.

The pose was ridiculous, the invitation grotesque. He didn't intend to laugh at her, but a snicker escaped him before he could smother it, and she sank back onto the bed.

"I'm sorry," he said. "I didn't mean to laugh."

"I thought we came here to have ourselves some fun. I thought we came here for my birthday. But you won't even fuck me."

"I've just got a lot on my mind," he said. "That's all."

She lay across the bed, her face pressed against the mattress. She clasped her hands and slipped them between her thighs. Her hair fell across her face.

"I know what it is," she cried. "It's still *her*, isn't it, cowboy?"

She fell asleep or passed out—he didn't know which. He pulled her hair back off her face. He could see the thin veins beneath her translucent skin.

Of course it was Liana. Darlene saw him more clearly than he could see himself—she saw what he had become. And when she woke and discovered that he had walked out on them, that he had ditched them after talking them into crossing the border, she would hate him as much as he had begun to hate himself.

He walked over to the fan in the window and directed it at her, then he pulled the sheet over her bare shoulders so she wouldn't catch a chill. He turned the light down so that she could see where she was if she woke before Marilyn returned. Her mouth would be dry. She would be dehydrated from the mescal. He moved into the bathroom and filled a glass with water, then left it on the nightstand for her.

He wanted to tell her what had happened. The urge to confess it all to her, even as she slept, nearly overcame him. It wouldn't matter if she heard or understood or even cared. Someday, he thought, he would write her a long letter and explain it all, but he knew how hollow those words would sound.

He took out his wallet. He had less than seventy dollars. He placed a twenty-dollar bill on the bureau. It wasn't much, but it would get them back across the border and home to Venice. It was all he could afford.

Marilyn was due back soon. He knew he had to be gone before she arrived. Darlene moaned, then stirred beneath the sheet, shrugging it off her shoulders. He watched her for a second, then slipped quietly out the door.

He crossed the courtyard and squatted down in the shadow of an old school bus jacked up on stacks of oil-soaked planks. Marilyn didn't make it back to the room for nearly an hour. She was accompanied by a middle-aged man in baggy khakis and a dark fedora. Like all her lovers, he was nearly a head shorter than she was. His white shirt was entirely unbuttoned, disclosing a rotund stomach covered with a savannah of black hair. He strayed as he walked, as if he were very drunk. She brought him back to her with a long arm.

"The light's still on," Marilyn said as they walked past the fountain. "They must still be partying."

Cahill watched them enter the room. The door closed. He waited a few minutes until the light went out, and then he was gone.

CHAPTER 17

THE NEXT DAY he caught a bus down the coast to Rosarito. The first night he was there he walked down to the old beach hotel. Through the tall white arch opening onto the landscaped grounds he could see the main entrance to the hotel. The stained glass above the carved wooden doors was filled with light from within the lobby. The whitewashed walls were lit by lamps mounted on the columns supporting the red-tiled roof. Arm in arm, a couple drifted through the gardens past the raised, ornately tiled flowerbeds.

The hotel didn't look to have changed since he and Liana had stayed there. He supposed it hadn't changed much since the days of Prohibition, when Americans were first lured down to Mexico to drink and gamble and seal their clandestine liaisons. Americans still dominated the town. Most were tourists, but there was also a community of expatriates with no interest at all in returning to the country they had fled.

For five days Cahill took refuge in their presence. He didn't go back to the hotel at all during that time. It would take a few days for the money from Steele to arrive. He couldn't risk arousing suspicion by asking about it too early or too often. All he could do was wait.

He rented a room above a pharmacy on the Boulevard de Benito Juarez, the town's main thoroughfare. The room had running water and door locks and cost just six dollars a night. From its lone window, he could look out across the tarpaper shacks below to the blue, subdued roll of the Pacific.

Everywhere he went he thought he saw Liana—following him through the crowded, open-roofed bars and along the dusty sidewalks, milling through the markets, stepping out of the curio shops into the blaze of the sun, even in the painted ceramic masks leering at him through the streaked, storefront windows. It drove him back to his room, where he lay on the bed fearing he might suffocate, as if all the oxygen had been scorched out of the air.

The nights he killed in a cantina called Pappagallo's, where the expatriates gathered beneath the watchful eyes of the retired Los Angeles cop who ran the place. With his back to the wall, Cahill sat alone at a table, nursing bottles of warm beer and watching the door. Every night at the stroke of midnight, a stripper named Magdalena showed up to grind out her act on the bar. Seated below, a knot of drunken men grabbed at her thick, dark legs, waving dollar bills she allowed them to shove brusquely inside her G-string.

Cahill asked no questions, and no one spoke to him—no one except a burly ex-football player named Monroe Givens. Everyone in Pappagallo's knew Givens. He had played tackle for the Oklahoma Sooners and then spent a year with the Detroit Lions. He was a huge man with a flat head and a full, biblical beard. After the Lions cut him, he'd gone to work in the shipyards in Long Beach, where several years ago, the long arm of a crane knocked a stack of wooden pallets onto him and another man. Three vertebrae in Givens's lower back were crushed. In what Givens viewed as a grievous injustice, the other man walked away unscathed.

For the next year Givens convalesced in a hospital bed, trapped inside a full body cast. As soon as he was released he fled to Mexico, where he knew his disability checks could sustain him in the manner he believed he deserved. He blamed the shipyard and the crane operator and, of course, the surgeons and doctors; he blamed the insurance company that refused to settle his claim and the lawyers he knew would bilk him for all he was worth if he were ever awarded a dime. Yet Givens had somehow reconciled himself to his life in Rosarito. His only disappointment or regret seemed to be the ubiquitous presence of the Mexicans.

He still required a cane to walk. It bowed beneath him as if it might snap as he made his way through the tables. Before he dropped down into the chair opposite Cahill, he shouted at the bartender to bring over a bottle of tequila. It arrived promptly, and he took a long slug. His brow furrowed as he set the bottle back down.

"Did you hear about that poor bastard down at Rosa's?"

Cahill shook his head, and Givens leaned forward so both his arms rested on the table.

"Rosa runs herself a whorehouse south of town," he said. He grinned broadly. "I'm not ashamed to admit I've introduced myself to a few of her girls. They're raised Catholic, most of them, which naturally puts a little fire in their loins.

"Well, this poor bastard goes down to Rosa's and asks her to see the girls. She looks him over and she tells him she's got something better than that as long as he's willing to pay a little extra. He thinks about it a minute and then figures what the hell; so Rosa leads him down the hall and lets him into this room. The minute he steps inside the door slams behind him. He spins around, and there's nothing there but this chicken."

Givens took another slug of tequila, then glanced back over his shoulder before continuing.

"So he stands there for a few minutes, sore

as hell and figuring he was had, but then he takes a look at the chicken and it lets out a little squawk, and he decides what the hell. He starts chasing it around the room until finally he grabs it, and then he starts fucking this chicken. I mean he's got its feet tucked into his pockets so he doesn't even have to hold onto it, and it's flapping its wings, and by God he likes it. Then all of a sudden Rosa opens the door and tells him that's it. His time's up, she tells him. The chicken's had enough for the day.''

Cahill smiled. He ran his hand back through his hair as Givens's chipped teeth flashed in a dark grin.

''All week he thought about that chicken,'' Givens said. ''He thought about that chicken all day long. He thought about that chicken as he climbed up on his tired old wife. He couldn't sleep at night. So at the end of the week he goes back to Rosa and asks her for the chicken, but she tells him no. He begs her, but she tells him no again. He gets down on his hands and knees. Finally she tells him she's got something better if he's willing to pay her fifty dollars, and I don't have to tell you he goes for it in a second.

''So she walks him down the same hall she took him before, past the room where she provided the chicken, then she lets him into another room. As he steps inside the door shuts behind him. This time there's just him and a guy with his face pressed up against the wall.

At first he wonders what this guy's doing, but then he sees he's looking through a peephole, so he steps up and takes a look for himself. In the next room are maybe a dozen women, buck naked and not a one of them under two hundred and fifty pounds, dancing around like ballerinas.

" 'What the fuck is this?' he asks the guy standing next to him. The guy pulls away from the peephole. 'I don't know,' he says. 'But last week we got to watch some idiot fuck a chicken!' "

Givens threw his head back and bayed with laughter. Cahill allowed himself a laugh too, though he was relieved no one else seemed to be paying much attention to them.

It took a minute for Givens to compose himself. He straightened in the chair as much as his spine would allow him, then he shoved the bottle of tequila across the table at Cahill.

"Go ahead," he said. "Take a drink. You look like you could use one."

Cahill wasn't sure exactly what Givens meant. After a minute he decided it didn't matter. He raised the bottle and took a swallow, then set it back down in front of Givens.

"You look like you're busted," Givens said.

"I've got money coming."

"I know when a man's dead broke," Givens said, as if it were a talent. "It's not so hard to tell."

Cahill reached out for the bottle again.

"What if this money doesn't come?"

"It'll come," Cahill said.

Givens studied him a minute. "I'll drink to that," he said.

Givens lived in a trailer on a bluff above the Pacific, not quite three miles south of Rosarito. He told Cahill he could spend the night on his floor if he wanted. Down to his last twenty dollars, Cahill was in no mind to turn him down.

As they pushed out of the cantina, Givens tossed his keys at Cahill, then waved his cane down the unpaved alley.

"It's a gold Barracuda," he said. "Bring it around and pick me up."

Cahill looked at Givens a moment, then started down the alley. He spotted the Barracuda at once. Scabs of rust grew along the creases on every panel of the body. The lid of the trunk was missing completely, and all the glass but the windshield had been broken out. The roof was caved in as if the car had been rolled.

Cahill slipped behind the wheel and started the car, then jabbed his finger at the push-button transmission on the dashboard and punched it into gear. He wheeled around and headed back toward the cantina. Givens was leaning on his cane in the green light cast by the neon parrot above the door. When Cahill pulled up in front of him, Givens lumbered unsteadily out to the car, then heaved himself into the seat.

"Go, man!" he shouted above the shrieking fan belt. "What the hell are you waiting on?"

Cahill headed for the road that led down the coast. As they drove through town Givens leaned out the window and screamed at two Mexicans walking down the street. To Cahill's immense relief they looked up and smiled, as if they recognized the Barracuda and accepted Givens's malice as the natural result of his injury.

With Givens exhorting him to go faster, they headed down the free road until Givens pointed up the side of the bluff, and they turned onto a rough dirt road marked by slabs of whitewashed shale. Cahill drove hard up the side of the mountain, the transmission dragging across the ridge between the ruts, the car sliding through each turn. The faster he drove, the louder Givens shouted his approval. When they finally reached the end of the road, the headlights shining through a gate in a chain-link fence, Givens seemed almost disappointed.

"You've got the keys," Givens said, pointing at the ignition, so Cahill climbed out of the car to unlock the gate.

Topped with three strands of barbed wire, the fence completely enclosed Givens's trailer, which was illuminated by the brilliant white light of an arc lamp. The trailer had been blue once, but constant exposure to the sun and the salt air had bleached the aluminum panels nearly white. In the far corner of the compound, a fifty-five-gallon drum lay on its side with unburned refuse spilling out the top. Mounted on a concrete pad, a huge black satellite dish aimed up into the sky.

Cahill slipped the key into the padlock that secured the gate. Suddenly two Dobermans boiled out from beneath the steps leading up to the trailer. They streaked toward him—he staggered backward as they hurled themselves at the gate.

"Down!" Givens shouted at them, whipping his cane across the hood of the car. "Get down, goddamnit!"

The instant the dogs recognized their master's gravelly voice they fell into a simpering disquiet. Then Givens began to cough. He doubled over. His face turned blue as if he was starving for oxygen. Finally he spat out a cord of phlegm and managed to catch his breath.

He straightened up and then waved his cane through the air.

"Open the fucking gate," he said.

They spent the rest of the night drinking and pitching horseshoes on the crusted ground. Before each throw Givens hitched up the black and blue plaid pants that clung to his waist without benefit of a ledge to grip, then he drew back his arm and slung the heavy shoe forward, holding his hand perfectly still as the shoe tumbled through the air and then clanked against the stake.

"I can't play without any money on the game," he declared. "I'm a gambling man. Otherwise I've got no concentration."

"I don't have any money," Cahill said, hoping that would end the discussion, but Givens was unfazed.

"I thought you said you had it coming," Givens said.

When Cahill didn't immediately respond, Givens stopped and turned to him.

"I do," Cahill said.

"Then we'll play for a hundred bucks a point," Givens said. "I'll keep the score."

As dawn broke and the first wisps of smoke began to rise from the shacks below, Cahill owed Givens more than ten thousand dollars.

"And you're gonna pay me every fucking cent," Givens growled as Cahill helped him into the musty trailer.

"I'll write you a check," Cahill said.

"No checks, no goddamn Mexican money neither," Givens said.

Cahill led him into the bedroom in the back and dropped him onto the bed.

"I deal strictly in cash."

"No problem," Cahill said.

* * *

In return for a place to stay, Cahill agreed to take the Barracuda into town to run several errands. It was a simple, three-stop trip that he accomplished easily before Givens hoisted himself out of bed late in the afternoon. He stopped first at the pharmacy to fill Givens's codeine prescription, then at a liquor store for beer and tequila, then he dropped by the post office to see if there was any new word in the lawsuits Givens had filed against all those he believed responsible for his back injury.

When he returned to the trailer, Givens swallowed a handful of the codeine capsules, chased them down with several cans of beer, then pitched the mail into the trash and staggered across the room to the couch, where he spent the rest of the day watching television. Cahill drank away his own hangover, but he felt trapped inside the trailer. He walked outside and stood at the fence and stared down at the glimmering ocean. Finally Givens raised himself from the couch and declared it was time to head down to Pappagallo's.

They sat at a table with two sailors down from San Diego. They were shipping out to Guam in the morning, and they'd come down to buy plaquettes of Quaaludes to help kill the long hours at sea. They were drinking up the nerve to smuggle them back across the border.

Givens regaled them with his stories about Mexican whores. When Magdelena arrived and performed on the bar in front of them, Givens's sadistic stories took on the unfortunate air of truth.

When the cantina finally closed, the sailors helped Cahill get Givens out to the Barracuda. While Cahill drove back down the coast to the trailer, Givens lay across the back seat, cursing the stars.

Cahill woke early the next morning and drove the Barracuda back into town. While waiting for Givens's codeine prescription to be filled, he noticed the pay phone in the back of the pharmacy. His mouth went dry; he wiped his face with his hand. It had never occurred to him to try to call Liana. His mind wheeled: he could tell her he'd made it, he could tell her he was waiting for her, he could tell her how sorry he was.

The girl behind the counter changed ten dollars into coins for him. He thanked her so exuberantly she took a wary step back from the cash register. He dialed the operator. Twice he was disconnected before she came on the line.

"I want to place a call to the States," he said, all but shouting into the receiver.

"I will try to reach the international operator," she said, and Cahill turned and leaned back against the wall and smiled broadly at the girl behind the counter.

He had to wait. His heart beat faster with each passing minute. Sweat trickled down from his armpits over his ribs. He shifted his weight from one leg to the other. He reached into his pocket and pulled out all his change and stacked the coins by denomination across the counter.

Finally he reached the international operator. Her voice was faint and distant; he had to shout the number of the ranch into the receiver. The girl behind the counter watched him carefully, her dark face expressionless.

But then he could hear it ringing. He raised his arm and wiped his forehead on the sleeve of his shirt. Suddenly he was terrified Liana would answer. He wanted to hang up before she picked up the receiver, before she knew it was him, before she saw how desperate he was. And yet he had to talk to her; he had to know if she was coming.

"Shall I keep trying?" the operator asked.

"Let it ring!" he shouted.

He knew she was there. He could feel her standing over the phone and watching it. She knew it was him. She had to know. Why didn't she pick it up?

"I'm sorry, sir," the operator said.

"No!"

"You'll have to place the call later," she said.

"No!" he shouted again, but then the line went dead.

"Goddamn you!"

He slammed the receiver down, then tried to jerk it off the body of the telephone. The cord snapped taut and pulled the receiver out of his hands. He kicked at it as it dangled against the wall.

Then he leaned against the wall, his forehead on the back of his arm, panting.

When he arrived back at the trailer, Givens announced he wanted to drive down to Ensenada to do some fishing.

They took the toll road and were there in a little over an hour. They rented a motorboat, a Chriscraft with a solid fiberglass hull and a Johnson outboard mounted on the transom, and took it out onto the Bahia de Todos Santos. While Cahill piloted the boat across the bay, Givens strapped himself into a swivel seat in the stern and cast a line into the water.

Before the day was over Givens had hooked two shimmering bonito, which Cahill, leaning over the gunwale, brought into the boat with a gaff. They were not the marlin or the sailfish Givens hoped to catch, but they put up a good fight and gave him a sense of triumph.

Eventually Givens's strength flagged in the sun, and he fell asleep. By the time Cahill got them back into port, Givens's pale flesh had been baked bright pink and his lips had begun to blister. Givens, naturally, didn't feel a thing.

On the way back up the coast, Givens spotted a young woman hitchhiking along the side of the toll road and ordered Cahill to pick her up. Cahill resisted him at first, but then he pulled over and she climbed into the back seat.

Her name was Leah. She had long brown hair. Peppered with freckles, her round, mousy face made her look no older than twenty, but as Cahill glanced up into the rearview mirror he could see the defeat swimming in her eyes and he knew she was considerably older than that.

She listened intently as Givens told her how he had been crippled in the shipyard in Long Beach. Givens could see she sensed the essence of his personal tragedy, and he invited her to spend the night with them. When they got back he took her directly to his bedroom.

In the middle of the night Cahill woke to her crying. She had stolen out of the bedroom and then had slipped out of the trailer and tried to leave. But the gate was locked, and she had dropped to the ground and curled up with her arms around her knees. Sitting on their lean, dark haunches, the two Dobermans watched her from across the compound.

"Are you all right?" Cahill asked as he helped her to her feet.

"I think so," she said, and he let her out.

He couldn't go back to sleep. A stale heat suffused the trailer. The awning above the door rattled in the uneven wind rising up the face of the bluff. He could hear Givens breathing through the open door to his bedroom. Fluid bubbled in his chest, deep in his congested lungs.

He pushed up off the blanket he'd spread

across the floor and dropped onto the couch. The girl had left a pack of cigarettes. He lit one and inhaled, but the menthol made him light-headed so he ground it out. All Liana wanted was time to sell the ranch. She knew they'd need the money. She'd promised to come down later. All he'd had to do was believe her. Now he realized she wasn't coming—she was never coming.

He got up. There was no reason to stay in Rosarito. The money from Steele had to have arrived at the hotel by now. The time had come to pick it up.

CHAPTER 18

HE DROVE THROUGH the white arch leading into the hotel grounds and then followed the cobbled road to the parking lot reserved for guests. As he climbed out of the Barracuda, he glimpsed himself in the rearview mirror. His own reflection startled him. His eyes were red and veined; the lines on his face had deepened to creases.

He got out of the car and tucked his shirt into his jeans. As he started toward the hotel he combed his hair with his fingers as best he could. The doors of the lobby were propped open to accept the cool morning air. As he stepped inside his boot heels struck a hollow cadence on the white tile floor.

"Sir, may I help you?" asked the clerk standing behind the desk. He wore a dark blue blazer. His voice was cleaned of accent or inflection.

Cahill crossed the lobby before responding. "I'm expecting a letter," he said quietly.

"The name, sir?"

"Winn Cahill."

The clerk turned away and stepped into the office behind the desk. Cahill shoved his hands into his pockets, then glanced over at a small man in a dark blue sports coat, sitting at a card table set up beneath a lurid mural of a tropical bay. The man was selling interests in a condominium project up the coast. He smiled at Cahill, then spread his thick, black moustache with his fingers.

The clerk returned with a bundle of envelopes bound with a thick rubber band and began thumbing through them.

"I'm sorry, sir," he said. "I don't seem to have anything for you, unless it might have come in late yesterday."

He snapped the rubber band around the letters, then bent down and glanced beneath the desk. "Oh yes," he said. "Here it is."

The clerk slid the letter across the blue tile. The instant Cahill spotted the Los Angeles postmark, he knew Steele had come through.

He carried the envelope through the hotel, into the bar that looked out onto the beach. No one was in the bar except the bartender, who was polishing martini glasses with a soft towel, and a middle-aged waitress in a short red dress.

She looked up and smiled as Cahill entered. He crossed the dance floor, then sat at one of the tables along the wall of windows. The sun flashed on the ocean. He could feel its heat through the salt-streaked glass.

The waitress came to him at once. She was a stout woman with black hair teased up in back and then sprayed into place. In her black high heels, she managed to look appreciably taller than her given height. The illusion seemed to please her.

"May I get you something?" she asked.

"Just a cup of coffee," he said.

He watched her walk away, brushing past the fronds of a potted palm on her way back to the bar. She returned immediately with his cup.

He dug the tip of a finger into the corner of the envelope from Steele, then worked it across the top and carefully ripped it open. He could see the bills inside. He withdrew the money and fanned it across the table. Immediately he saw that something was wrong. He checked the envelope again; he counted the bills a second time.

Then he laughed and rocked back in his chair. He couldn't believe it. Steele had sent him a hundred and fifteen dollars.

He reached for the cup of coffee. It rattled on the saucer as he picked it up. He raised the cup to his mouth and took a sip. The coffee splashed over the lip of the cup as he set it back down.

The waitress came over to him and placed a hand on his shoulder. "Are you all right?" she asked.

He smiled gamely at her.

She turned and looked back across the room. An old Mexican in a smart black tuxedo had just come into the bar; he sat at a table across the room. He had balding temples and a priestly face that had aged into sorrow.

"He is the piano player," she said. "I will ask him to play for you."

Cahill caught her arm. "No," he said.

"He is very good. He knows all the songs."

"Please," he said.

Then he turned and looked out the window. He couldn't believe Steele could get only a hundred and fifteen dollars for the Stratocaster and the amp. Or maybe he hadn't hawked the guitar at all. Something must have happened. Steele knew the money wouldn't last him two weeks.

He had no idea what to do next. He couldn't stay in Rosarito. For an instant he thought about taking Givens's Barracuda across the peninsula to San Felipe. There he could take a boat across the Sea of Cortez to the mainland. But the plan was thin, pointless. No matter where he went, he didn't have enough money to survive for long.

Then the piano began to play, a brittle Mexican folksong. Cahill turned around. The waitress beamed at him, her face as red and bright as a waxed apple; he wanted to kill her.

He looked back out the window. The sun nearly blinded him. He shaded his eyes with his hand and gazed out upon the long, sweeping beach. Gulls soared overhead, their wings outstretched as they settled upon the sand.

He watched the sleek white sailboats down from the States glide past the tankers moored off the oil refinery north of town. Maybe he could catch a ride down the coast on one of the sailboats. The possibility excited him and for a moment gave him hope. But then he realized it wasn't going to happen. Again he despaired.

Then he saw her.

He leapt to his feet, his thighs crashing into the table, spilling the coffee. He squinted into the blaze of the sun.

With one hand she gathered up her dress as she walked through the foaming surf. The other hand clung to a floppy white hat. She was no more than two hundred yards down the beach.

He shoved the money into his pocket, then ran out of the bar. He ran down the steps and then across the grass to the gate that opened onto the beach. He shouted her name, but she couldn't hear him above the crashing waves. She didn't see him as he sprinted out onto the sand behind her.

Then he stopped. Suddenly he remembered the thousands of times he'd been sure he'd seen her before, each a mirage, a delusion, a cruel trick he played on himself; he couldn't stand it again, the agony of discovering it wasn't her—not again, not this time, not here.

Somehow she sensed him standing behind her. She whirled around to him, then burst into tears.

"Dear Jesus," she cried. "Just look at you."

CHAPTER 19

HE WAS AFRAID to open his eyes, as if he might discover she wasn't really there. He leaned back in the tub and could hear her rinsing out the razor. Then he listened to the blade draw across his face, through the stubble she'd softened with a warm wet towel.

"I got here late last night," she said. "I flew down to Los Angeles and then took a bus to Tijuana and then I took a cab down the coast. The driver couldn't have been fifteen years old. He was driving this yellow station wagon that looked like it had been painted with a broom. I thought he was going to drive us off the cliff."

She dragged the razor around the rim of his jaw, then stopped. She dabbed at him with a towel. "I've cut you," she said. "You're bleeding."

He couldn't feel it. He opened his eyes. With her hair loosely knotted at the back of her head, she was kneeling beside the tub in the cottage she had rented on the beach below the hotel. He still couldn't believe she was there with him;

he couldn't believe he'd spotted her on the beach. He was not accustomed to such good luck and was naturally predisposed not to trust it.

Liana tossed the razor up into the sink, then she sat back against the bathroom wall, her legs stretched out before her on the puddled tile.

"You look so much better now," she said. "You look like a new man."

"I called you," he said. "I finally got through to the ranch, but you never answered."

She looked down at her lap. "I thought it was you—I knew it was you," she said. "But I couldn't answer. I was just getting ready to leave. David Earle wouldn't let me. He was afraid the telephone might be tapped."

"I didn't know what the hell was going on. I didn't know what to think." He took a deep breath. He could see himself in her bedroom, his arm drawn back, his hand clenched into a fist; he could feel the rage coursing through him as he hurled her to the floor.

"I didn't mean to hurt you."

She allowed herself to smile at him. "You didn't hurt me."

He watched as she reached up and untied her hair and let it fall to her shoulders.

"Where did you get that hat?" he asked her.

"Oh, Faith gave it to me—and I was foolish enough to wear it. She gave it to me to protect against the sun."

"She knows where we are?"

"She knows we're in Mexico."

"Who else?"

She looked at him, startled by the question, as if he were accusing her of something.

"Only David Earle."

She came to him and dabbed at his neck with the towel. She ran her hand over his forehead, over his wet hair.

"What are you worried about them for?" she asked. "I'm here. We're together, aren't we? That's what you want, isn't it?"

Her body gleamed as she lay across the bed. The room was nearly dark, the curtains drawn against the light, sealing them off from the outside world. Sweat tracked down to the swale along her spine, pooling in the small of her back where the faintest whorl of soft blond hair swept down onto her buttocks.

The bed groaned as Cahill pushed up and padded barefoot across the room. They had been asleep for hours, clutching each other despite the relentless heat.

He sat in one of the chairs arranged around the table. The varnished surface was scarred with rings left by moist bottles and glasses. It rocked on the uneven floor as he leaned onto it.

Liana rolled onto her back. Her chest rose and fell with each breath of the tepid air. Her hair snaked across the white sheets.

"I want to go to New Orleans," she said. "I

went there with my mother once. We took the bus and met Lester there. It was a horrible trip. Every stop Clarisse would get off the bus and buy a bottle of orange soda. She'd suck a little soda out, then fill the bottle back up with vodka. She got sick in Texas—I don't remember where exactly. She was sick all the way back. No one would sit anywhere near us.''

Then she stared dreamily up at the ceiling. ''New Orleans is old and beautiful. I remember lying in bed and listening to the radio. I listened all night—first to some jazz, then to a gospel station. You can just go down the dial.''

She pushed up to look at him. ''We can't stay here,'' she said. ''Not forever.''

Cahill rubbed his neck, still raw from the razor. ''There's the small matter of crossing back into the States,'' he said, but she seemed not even to hear him.

''It's a matter of time and place—when and where.''

He reached across the table for her black leather handbag. ''I want to take a look at the new I.D.,'' he said.

Liana fell back onto the bed and draped an arm over her eyes. ''It's in there,'' she said impatiently, as if annoyed with him for not sharing her enthusiasm about New Orleans.

He found the envelope and lifted the flap, then spread out the pieces of identification across the table as if he were dealing himself a hand of solitaire—a driver's license, social security card, voter registration card, several credit cards. He picked up the driver's license and examined the photograph of himself.

"Where did David Earle get all this?" he asked.

Liana shrugged. "Faith said he knew somebody—one of his clients, I think."

He marveled at the identification's veneer of authenticity. "How did you decide on Thomas Starr?"

"I think it's a handsome name," she said. "Don't you like it?"

"I like it fine."

"Mine is Joanna Douglas."

She sat up. "Faith and I went down to the courthouse," she said. "We looked through the death certificates until we found people our age. That way we can send for their birth certificates like they were our own.

"You were born in Las Vegas. Your birthday is December twenty-eighth. I don't know when you moved to California, but you drowned. It was a boating accident in the river. Faith and I looked it up in the newspaper in the library.

"I was born in Chicago, Illinois, on March fifteenth—the Ides of March. We moved to Loma Roja when I was only seven years old. We lived on Eighth Street, near the water tower. Then one day the house burned down. My mother died too. The death certificate listed the cause of death as total incineration."

Cahill shook his head, then shoved the I.D. back into the envelope.

"Did you register here as Joanna Douglas?"

"Of course I did," she said. "That's who I am now."

The new Thomas Starr stood up and walked to the window. He pulled the curtain back and squinted into the fierce red eye of the sun.

He could live with his new name, but he didn't know what to think about New Orleans. With the money from the ranch they could go where they wanted. It would last longest in Mexico, but Liana was right—they couldn't stay here forever. They'd end up like Givens, isolated and afraid, at once indulged and despised by the locals.

Liana rose behind him. She slipped her arms around his waist, then pressed against his back.

On the beach a Mexican man in a bulky brown overcoat and dark leather hat was squatting in an old car seat propped up in the shade of a slab of concrete. Already saddled, three old mares stood idly on the hot sand, clipped to a line strung between two posts, their long tails slapping across their haunches.

"Let's go for a ride on the beach," she said.

He turned to her.

"Please?"

They walked down to the horses. The man in the overcoat rose from the car seat and walked out to them, shuffling his sandals through the cratered sand.

"Do you wish to take these fine horses for a ride along the beach?" He waved his hand across the sky. "This is the most beautiful time of day."

Liana looked sadly at the horses. "I feel sorry for them," she said.

Cahill walked down the line strung between the two posts. "How much?" he asked, raising his voice above the surf.

"Two dollars per hour," the man said, grinning through a mouth of black teeth. "Each," he added, as if an afterthought. "These are very fine horses, the finest horses on the beach."

"You don't feed them," Liana said, turning to face him. "They've been standing in the sun all day. You haven't even given them any water."

The man looked emptily at her, puzzled by the accusation. "They are beautiful, no?"

Cahill stepped up as if to intercede. "I'll give you a dollar each," he said.

The man snatched the money out of Cahill's hand, then smiled broadly at Liana. "Which of these fine horses would you like to ride?"

The three horses shifted anxiously as he approached them. When the chestnut mare at the end snorted and tried to rear back onto its hind legs, the man grabbed the reins and tugged down sharply.

"I'll take her," Liana said, as if beckoned by its fear.

"She is a very fine horse," the man assured her.

Cahill pointed at the dark mare beside her, and the man untied them both. Liana took the reins from him, then swung up into the saddle.

"You will find this horse to your liking, I am sure," the man said to her.

As Cahill climbed up onto his horse it took a sudden step to the left as if it meant to bolt down the beach, but he drew back sharply on the reins and then stroked the side of its neck, and it settled down.

"Are you ready?" he asked Liana.

When she nodded, he gently spurred his horse's flanks. It lurched forward, then fell into a brooding, dispirited walk. When he glanced back at Liana, he saw she hadn't moved. The mare's head hung down nearly to the sand, its knotted mane spilling down its broad neck. She pulled back on the reins and spurred it again with the heels of her boots. Still she couldn't coax it to move.

She didn't see the Mexican running up to the mare from behind. Before Cahill realized what he intended to do, the Mexican picked up a plank leaning against the far post and then swung it across the mare's haunches, splintering the board into pieces.

The mare lifted her head only slightly, as if neither surprised nor hurt by the blow. The man bent down to retrieve the longest piece of the plank, but before he could pick it up, Liana jumped down in front of him.

"What are you doing?" she shouted at him.

Startled, the Mexican glanced down at the sand, as if to move toward the piece of plank again, but Liana planted herself directly in his path. He backed away from her, his hands extended to either side as if he had no idea why she was so angry. When she shook her head disgustedly at him, he broke into wild laughter, both terrified and amused by her.

"Get away from her!" Liana shouted, waving him away with both her hands.

Cahill watched him walk back up the beach to his car seat, where the man pulled down the brim of his hat as if to ignore them completely.

Cahill dismounted, then led his horse back to Liana. She reached down and took the reins and lifted the mare's head. She inspected the bridle and bit, then circled her horse, examining it carefully. She pointed at two bare patches of skin on the mare's forelegs, just below its knees.

"It looks like she ran into something, like a piece of wire, or maybe she was trying to jump a fence," she said.

She brushed the side of the mare's neck. "But she looks all right," she said.

"What do you want to do?" Cahill asked.

"Maybe if we just walk them for a while," she said.

* * *

After they had walked several hundred yards down the beach, Liana lifted herself back into the saddle. She leaned down and clicked her tongue in the mare's ear, then spurred it into an easy pace.

They rode down to the water and galloped through the surf, then they rode down the beach until they stopped to watch the sun slide into the ocean. The sky turned gunmetal blue.

On the crest of a bluff above the high reaches of the beach rose a small wooden cross. He nodded at it, and Liana turned.

"Let's go take a look," she said.

They rode over to the base of the bluff, then dismounted and scrambled up through the rock. The cross was made of two bleached pieces of driftwood crudely wired together and then driven into the ground at the head of a grave marked by pieces of rock.

"It's so small," Liana said.

"Maybe it's a dog," Cahill said.

"You wouldn't bury a dog here, not looking out over the ocean," she said. "Maybe it's somebody's baby, somebody poor who couldn't afford a proper funeral."

She dropped down onto both knees beside it. Cahill watched her for a moment, then looked up into the hills to the east. A fire burned between two shacks. He could hear the horses snorting on the beach below.

"Let's go," he said.

He started back down through the rocks. "Come on, before it gets dark."

Liana pushed up and stood above the grave. The wind rippled her blouse and tossed her hair. Shadows collected in the hollows of her cheeks. "Shouldn't we pray or something?"

"If you want to, Liana."

"I'll say a prayer."

"Pray for all of us," he said.

They rode back to the hotel, then returned to the cottage. Liana had brought his clothes from Loma Roja. They were washed and pressed and neatly folded into a brown leather suitcase that had belonged to Francis Robert. As he dressed for dinner he found a note from Faith in the pocket of his pants. "Be careful," was all it said.

Liana wore a long, light blue strapless dress that drew in at her waist and passed smoothly over her hips. On a silver necklace a cameo clung to her dark skin. The salt air charged her hair.

They had dinner in the hotel dining room, looking out on the pool. A man with a shock of white hair and a dark blue blazer sat at the table beside them. Flanked by his wife and her two chattering sisters, the man stared at Liana throughout the dinner. Even as they left, Cahill caught him glancing back at her. He looked distantly familiar, though Cahill had no idea where he might have seen him before. It made him nervous. For the first time he realized how much he had to lose.

After dinner they moved into the bar, where several dozen people were dancing in front of the piano. They sat at the table along the window where he had spotted her that morning. The crashing of the waves was dim and distant, lost to the music of the piano player, who had nodded circumspectly at Cahill as he and Liana entered.

Liana drank champagne, but it made her melancholy.

"Someday I want a child," she said. "We'll name him Winn. He'll have your hair and your eyes, but he'll be left-handed like me. Before you know it girls will be calling on the telephone and asking for him. When we get to New Orleans I'm going to see a doctor."

He led her onto the dance floor and slipped both arms around her waist and drew her up to him. She wrapped her arms around his neck and rested her head against his chest. As they glided across the dance floor, he could feel her tears soaking through his shirt.

When they returned to the cottage, Cahill built a fire in the white hearth across the room. Outside the window, the wind rustled the palms. They could hear the surf washing across the shore.

Liana sat on the edge of the bed, staring into

the crackling flames. Cahill rose from in front of the hearth and joined her.

"Did Mooney ever come out to the ranch?" he asked.

"After you left he came out," she said. "He was looking for you. I told him I didn't know where you were."

"Did he believe you?"

She shrugged. "I don't know," she said. "Then he came out yesterday, or maybe it was the day before. He said they found the Mustang in Los Angeles. I told him I didn't know anything about that. I told him I hadn't seen you or heard from you."

She sighed, as if recalling events that had transpired deep in the past. "He asked about that night," she said, and suddenly her eyes filmed with tears. "I told him you killed Tommy. I had to. What else could I say? All I was trying to do was to get down here."

Cahill took a deep breath, then slipped his arm around her. She rested her head on his shoulder. He didn't blame her; he knew it was something she'd had to do.

"It's all right, Liana."

"You forgive me?"

"Sure I do."

They made love by the primitive light of the fire. Afterward he lay beside her and held her in his arms until she finally fell asleep.

He got up carefully and walked over to the

table and rifled through her bag until he located her wallet. Inside he found the new Illinois driver's license Wagner had procured for her. The name Joanna suited her well, even if for no reason other than it sounded so much like her given name. He wouldn't have chosen Thomas Starr for himself, but it didn't bother him. It was clean and simple, like the break he knew they had to make from what they had done.

His pants hung over the back of one of the chairs. He slipped his wallet out of the pocket and removed his old identification cards from the clear plastic leaves, then carried them over to the hearth. Piece by piece, he tossed them into the fire. They fluttered onto the glowing coals, burst swiftly into flame, then curled into ash.

He turned and looked at Liana. He wondered what New Orleans would be like, but as he slipped his new identification into the leaves of his wallet, he couldn't imagine it. All he knew was that the Mississippi River emptied into the Gulf of Mexico nearby. He supposed that would be something to see when they got there.

He tossed another branch onto the fire, sending a shower of sparks up the flue, then returned to the table. Even if Mooney had already figured out they'd fled to Mexico, even if he'd already alerted the Mexican authorities, no one would expect them to cross back into the States—at least not so soon. He spread the road map out across the table. In the trembling light, he traced the highway to Mexicali and then along the border to Nogales. No one would ever look for them to turn up there. At Nogales they would cross into Arizona. From there they would make their way down to New Orleans, where Joanna Douglas and Thomas Starr would see about having a child.

That night he dreamed they were in Nogales. There was a church with a bell in its adobe spire. Beside the church a small fenced cemetery was populated with tilted headstones. A grove of fruit trees had been planted beyond it.

An ancient priest with a leathery face lived in the adjacent rectory. In his white robe he was standing in front of the dark wooden doors, his arms outstretched, welcoming them. He leaned into the door with his frail, tired frame and swung it back. They followed him inside.

Liana was wearing a new white gown. He'd bought it for her with the money Steele had sent. She cradled a bouquet of roses in her arms. The church was cool and quiet and utterly at rest, and there in the refracted light they stood before the altar, and he vowed to love her and cherish her and not until death would they part.

CHAPTER 20

CAHILL PULLED BACK the sliding glass door and stepped out onto the patio, where Liana was reclining in a lounge chair. Her hair was wet from her bath. Combed out, it clung tightly to her skull. Her robe fell away from her legs, extended to the morning sun.

He handed her the cup of coffee he'd brought down from the dining room. She set it on the table beside her. "You're a dear," she said.

Then she turned her face toward the sky, her eyes hidden behind dark glasses. Cahill looked up at the hotel. A row of palms towered above the glass wall that enclosed the pool. Their fronds filled like fans in the breeze picking up from the beach. Already the sun had risen directly overhead, the position it seemed to maintain all day, as if to deny the barren landscape even the promise of shade.

"I have to return a car," he said.

"What car?"

"It's out front. It's an old Barracuda. I borrowed it from a guy named Givens."

"How long will that take?"

"Not long," Cahill said. "He lives just down the coast."

"You had it all night?"

"Let's just say your arrival distracted me from the business at hand."

She lifted her sunglasses up onto her forehead. "This Givens isn't going to be mad?"

"He'll be mad, all right. He's always mad. I'll buy him a case of beer. That'll shut him up."

"Maybe I should come along to protect you."

Cahill laughed. "I like that idea," he said.

They passed through the hotel lobby, then walked out into the courtyard. A man and a woman emerged from the curio shop across the courtyard, scolding each other for paying such a high price for a ceramic urn. Beside the shop a young Mexican boy stood on the top rung of a wooden ladder that was propped up against the smooth gray trunk of a palm. A man who looked to be his father steadied it from below. Cahill watched as the boy sawed off one of the dried fronds; it crashed loudly on the cobbled pathway.

They walked out to the parking lot where the Barracuda was parked amid the Buicks and Lincolns down from the States, gleaming like they'd just been driven off the showroom floor. As he opened the door of the Barracuda, he saw that a plastic bag filled with empty beer bottles had been pitched into the lidless trunk.

"Who is this Givens who loaned you his car?" Liana asked as she slid in beside him.

"He's an American. He lives down here."

He started the car, then turned to her. "I met him in a bar. He let me stay on the floor of his trailer for a few days."

They pulled out of the parking lot, then drove past the white-painted trunks of the palms that lined the road leading out of the hotel. Cahill reached over and patted the top of her thigh.

"Don't worry," he said.

He waited for an opening in the traffic cruising past on the Boulevard de Benito Juarez, then stomped down hard on the accelerator. The tires squealed on the oil-slicked brick as they headed back into town.

When he spotted a liquor store he pulled off to the edge of the street and parked alongside the raised sidewalk. Two men wearing soiled blue baseball caps were talking beneath the corrugated tin awning above the door. Strung across the white cinder-block facade, a banner advertising beer for sale by the case sloughed in the breeze.

"You can wait here if you want," he said, but Liana had already opened the car door.

They walked into the store. Bottles of tequila and Mexican wine were sparsely arranged on the shelves. Cases of beer were stacked up in the middle of the concrete floor. He lifted one of the cases from the stack and carried it to the counter, where the owner stood over his metal cash box. He was a small, wiry man. Black hair spilled out the neck of his sleeveless white T-shirt. His left eye wandered off to the side as if it had a mind of its own.

As Cahill set the beer down the owner nodded at him, then reached up to the stub of a pencil tucked behind his ear.

"I thought you sold the beer by the case," Cahill said, uncertain why it was necessary to calculate the price.

The owner slapped an open palm on the box. Dust exploded from the seams. "Twenty-four bottles of beer," he said. "This I guarantee."

Cahill nodded without further protest. As he handed the man a twenty-dollar bill, he wondered why he had bothered to say anything at all to him. He didn't care how much the beer cost. All he wanted was to assuage Givens's anger. The beer would be worth that at any price.

As the owner counted out his change, laying down the pesos and dollars as if they were interchangeable currency, Cahill turned to Liana. "Maybe we should get a bottle of tequila," he said. "It's a long bus ride to New Orleans."

Liana smiled at him as if the thought gave her a lift. "You think of everything, don't you, Thomas Starr?"

Cahill motioned at the bottles on the wall behind the counter. "I'll take one of those, too," he said.

The owner reached up and placed one of the bottles on the counter. Cahill picked it up. He raised it to the sun slanting through the open door. The light cast bands of color across his forearm.

Then he spotted the police car pulling up in front of the liquor store.

"Liana," he said quietly.

She turned; he nodded toward the door. Blue, with dark gray mud streaking out from around the wheel wells, the police car stopped directly behind the Barracuda.

"What do they want?" she asked as she moved behind the cases of beer.

Suddenly Cahill realized that Givens must have reported the car stolen.

He set the bottle on the counter, then stepped back into the shadows, out of view. Through the window, he watched as the policeman unfolded himself from behind the wheel of his car, then walked around to look at the Barracuda. His arms and shoulders filled the sleeves of his light blue uniform. He had a solemn, joyless face with a dark broom of a moustache.

"Jesus," Cahill sighed.

He turned to Liana just in time to see her fleeing through the back door.

"Wait!"

Instinctively he moved after her. The owner shouted for him to stop. Cahill spun around into the barrel of a pistol braced with both hands across the counter.

"No!" Cahill shouted, raising his hands above his head.

He glanced out the front door. His service revolver drawn, the policeman leaned across the roof of the car, shouting into the car radio.

A bottle exploded on the shelf behind Cahill. Fired by the owner, a second slug skipped off the floor as Cahill hurled himself headlong at the door. He rolled across the concrete, then into the alley. The instant he hit the ground, he scrambled to his feet and took off running.

Liana was already well down the alley, slipping past a bobtail truck parked behind a restaurant. The canvas door had been tossed up onto the roof of the truck. Slabs of meat hung on hooks inside; pale yellow carcasses rose up to the knees of two young Mexican boys inside.

When Cahill reached the truck he glanced back toward the liquor store. The policeman who had spotted the Barracuda burst out the back door.

Liana screamed. Ahead, another police car turned into the alley, sealing it off. Two policemen threw open the doors of the car, then took cover behind them. Liana ran back toward Cahill, pounding on the back door of the restaurant, then trying the door of the adjacent pharmacy. Over a bullhorn, a voice shouted in Spanish, then in English, for them to stop.

She was gone. Cahill ran after her. She'd found a narrow gap between the pharmacy and the restaurant, barely wide enough to pass through. He squeezed in after her.

By the time he reached the sunlight at the other end of the space between the buildings, Liana was running down the unpaved street fully a hundred yards ahead of him. She cut through an open market with dozens of baskets and clay pots arranged across the compacted soil, then turned into the barrio spilling down to the beach.

Shrieking and laughing as if it were a game, children dashed through the street and then chased after her. Old women with wrinkled mahogany faces squatted in the low doorways, watching first Liana and then Cahill race past, amused by the spectacle of a man running after a woman.

Suddenly a police car cut in front of Cahill, skidding to a stop on the loose gravel and dirt. He threw his hands in the air as two policemen exploded out the doors.

"This is all a mistake!" he shouted.

A second police car pulled up behind him. Cahill turned as the policeman who had spotted the Barracuda climbed out.

"I can explain!" he shouted.

He never saw the nightstick that dropped him from behind. Stunned, he tried to push back up. A boot on the shoulder stomped him back down. Then he was kicked in the ribs, so hard he came up off the ground. As he rolled away, another boot kicked him squarely in the face.

Then the policeman was kneeling down in front of him, pressing the barrel of his revolver to his forehead, shouting in such fierce Spanish that Cahill couldn't understand a word. He tried to peer through his arms, now raised to cover his face, but all he could see was the white-hot vortex of the sun.

He felt himself reeling. He felt himself lifting off the ground and spiraling toward the sun; he felt its intense heat on his face.

He cried out Liana's name, and then he felt nothing at all.

CHAPTER 21

THE ROOM SEEMED to rise up out of itself. An electric fan drew a long, flat wisp of cigarette smoke across the room, then sent it through the wire mesh screen bolted over the window. Beneath the window, sheets of green plaster were flaking off the wall, baring the cinder block underneath.

In a blue uniform nearly soaked through with sweat, a police captain named DeLeon was sitting behind a large wooden desk. He was a stocky, thickly muscled man with gold-capped teeth. His wavy black hair was combed back across his scalp. Trimmed to two thin lines, his moustache slanted across his broad upper lip.

A wave of nausea closed over Cahill. His vision seemed to dissolve, and he felt himself blacking out again, but then a hand at the back of his neck grabbed his shirt and jerked him upright in the chair.

His right eye was swollen shut. He could feel the fluid draining out of the corner of it, then crusting on his cheek and around his mouth. A searing pain filled the upper right side of his chest. His wrists were cuffed so tightly his hands were numb. One by one, they pressed his fingers on the ink pad, then rolled them across a small card until they had a complete set of prints.

With his feet kicked up onto one of the desk drawers, DeLeon rocked back and forth in his chair. He was casually inspecting the identification from Cahill's wallet, tossing each piece onto the desk as if he were flipping playing cards into an upturned hat.

"You are from Las Vegas?" he asked. "You live on Myrtle Street? Tell me, what is a myrtle? A myrtle is like a turtle?" he asked, provoking a hearty laugh from the policeman holding Cahill up.

"I don't think we have these myrtles here in Rosarito. At least I do not know them."

He opened the wallet, then rocked forward and spread the money Steele had sent across the desk. "You are here on vacation?"

It required all of Cahill's strength to nod.

"You do not have very much money for an American on vacation. Who was this woman you ran from the liquor store with?"

"I never saw her before," Cahill said, his voice so low and hoarse he scarcely recognized it as his own.

"You are traveling alone?" DeLeon asked.

He nodded.

"It is a shame to be alone in such a beautiful city as Rosarito," DeLeon said.

He looked up at Cahill. "Perhaps you met someone here. Perhaps you care for her a great deal and do not wish to involve her." DeLeon wagged a finger at Cahill and smiled, his gold teeth glinting. "I think this is true," he said.

He rose from behind his desk, then crossed the room and gazed out the mesh screen. He withdrew a blue plastic comb from his back pocket and dragged it back through his hair.

"Do you know why you are here, Mr. Starr? You are under arrest for stealing a vehicle belonging to a Mr. Monroe Givens. You know Mr. Givens, do you not?"

"I know him," Cahill said.

"Yes, I know you do," DeLeon said. "It is a grave offense to steal a vehicle belonging to another man."

DeLeon slipped the comb back into his pocket, then ran his fingertips across his eyebrows, smoothing them.

"Mr. Givens contacted us last night to report his vehicle missing. He said an American had been staying with him. He said this American had stolen his vehicle.

"I told Mr. Givens to wait, that perhaps this American would think twice about his actions and return it. Mr. Givens is not a patient man, as you are aware, but I was able to persuade him to give our methods a chance to work.

"But then this morning Officer Hernandez

here spotted Mr. Givens's vehicle outside the liquor store. You were inside, I believe."

"I borrowed the car," Cahill tried to explain. "I stopped at the liquor store to buy some beer to take to him."

But DeLeon seemed not to hear him. He returned to his desk and picked up Cahill's driver's license. He smiled warmly.

"Tell me about this Las Vegas," he said. "I have heard about it. I have heard it is never dark there, day or night, any time of the year. Are you employed there?"

Cahill stared at him, tilting his head as if to see him more clearly with his left eye. "I work at one of the casinos."

DeLeon laughed. "You are a gambler?"

"A pit boss."

It puzzled DeLeon. "What is this pit boss?"

"The pit boss supervises the dealers."

DeLeon's face developed a smile. "They have trusted you with an important job."

Cahill didn't say anything. He felt like he was losing altitude, sinking into the chair. Abruptly he was jerked back up from behind.

"This is what troubles me," DeLeon said, shaking his head. "You are a trusted man, down from Las Vegas. You are traveling through Rosarito on vacation alone, yet you have so little money that you must sleep on Mr. Givens's floor. Then you try to steal Mr. Givens's vehicle."

"You've got it all fucked up," Cahill said.

"Who was the woman in the liquor store with you?"

"I told you I never saw her before."

"What was her name?"

"I don't know."

DeLeon reached across his desk for a pack of cigarettes. He struck a match, lit a cigarette, then waved the match out.

"Would it surprise you to know that we are looking for this woman as part of our investigation?"

Cahill stared emptily at him.

DeLeon rose from his desk. "We will find her," he said. "She will turn up. Perhaps you will remember her name. Perhaps you will remember where you first met her. I am sure you will find time to think about her."

The cell was small, as cramped as a cage. Its walls were covered with initials and dates left by those who had suffered there before him. A single bare bulb burned dimly in the ceiling above the two metal bunks shoved up against opposite walls. The mattresses were rank with sweat. The matting inside had coagulated into clumps.

He knew he was hurt. He reached across his chest with his left arm and carefully probed his ribs. The pain was centered high, almost to his armpit. He worried his lung might have been punctured when they kicked him.

But mostly he worried about his eye. He had

tried to pull up his right eyelid, but it was stretched taut over his eye as if fused to the cornea itself. The entire side of his face ached. The bone around the socket burned as if it were on fire.

He lay back, arms at his sides, measuring out each breath. He couldn't believe Liana hadn't been caught. Somehow she had disappeared into the barrio. Maybe someone had helped her. Maybe she was still there, lying low, waiting to slip away.

Or maybe she was gone. The thought panicked him. Suddenly his blood felt like it was boiling in his veins. He felt like he was going to burst into flame.

She was his only chance. No one else even knew where he was. She couldn't just leave him there.

They had to hold him down to give him the shot. Hernandez, the policeman who'd spotted the Barracuda at the liquor store, plunged the needle into his arm, then jerked it out.

They held him down until the morphine came over him. After a minute they released him. A trickle of blood ran out of the mark in his arm. He didn't move.

He could see himself below, lying on the bunk, as if he had lifted out of his body. A liquid warmth spread over him; he felt secure, insulated, adrift.

There was no pain. He felt nothing at all. Time eluded him entirely. He had no idea how long he had been lying on the bunk, yet he was content to remain there indefinitely. The needle-mark in his arm had been joined by another. A deep blue bruise occupied the crook of his arm. He didn't really care.

Vaguely he heard voices. At first they seemed to have no origin. Then he heard a sharp rapping sound, like a stick dragged across a storm drain. He awakened to it, gradually coming to realize the voices were in the corridor outside the door of his cell. He lifted his head to see about the noise, who it was.

"That's him," Givens growled, his hoary face filling the window in the door.

It amused Cahill no end.

Later they came for him in the cell. Hernandez and another policeman gripped him under his arms, then raised him up and helped him down the corridor to DeLeon's office. They sat him down hard in the chair across DeLeon's desk. This time they didn't bother to cuff his wrists.

By the sunlight angling through the wire mesh screen, he guessed it was late in the afternoon. He had no idea what day it was. A trail of dried blood led out of a new needlemark in his arm.

Someone had wrapped a cloth around his head. He reached up and could feel a pad of gauze underneath, over the eye. The fluid leaking out of it had thickened. Absorbed by the gauze, it had begun to smell. He felt like he was beginning to decompose.

DeLeon was cleaning the dirt out from beneath his fingernails with a pocketknife. His glossy hair shone.

"We are very disappointed with you," he said without looking up.

"I believe you know what I am talking about."

Cahill stared emptily across the room. Cramps seized his emptied stomach, nearly doubling him over.

"Have you thought about this woman who is with you?" he asked. "I'm sure you have. Who is she?"

Cahill shook his head. He wasn't going to give her up; it was all the dignity that remained to him.

"It is to your advantage to tell us," DeLeon said.

DeLeon folded the blade back into its handle, then slipped it into his pocket. He opened the drawer of his desk and removed Cahill's wallet. He slipped the driver's license from its plastic sheath.

"We were able to contact the authorities in your Las Vegas. I placed the call myself. They have informed me that Thomas Starr has never been issued a Nevada driver's license such as this. They have suggested to me that this driver's license of yours is not authentic."

He dropped the license onto the desk, then leaned back in his chair.

"I was sure they were wrong. I was sure you would not lie to an officer of the law such as myself. But perhaps I misjudged you. Perhaps you are not the man you say you are.

"This is why we have sent your fingerprints to the federal marshall in your San Diego. We must find out who you are. There is a reason you call yourself Thomas Starr. We shall see."

Cahill turned his arms out for DeLeon to see the tracks and bruises. Barely able to hold up his head, he pleaded, "I need a doctor."

The cloth around his head slipped down slightly over his left eye; he could barely see out from beneath it.

DeLeon's eyes were as black as iron.

"You have seen a qualified medical authority," he said. "You were examined the day before yesterday."

Weakly, Cahill shook his head; he didn't remember it at all.

"Your eye," DeLeon said, looking up at Hernandez. "I am sorry to say it does not look good. This is the price you must pay for resisting arrest in Rosarito."

CHAPTER 22

WAGNER ARRIVED THREE days later. In blue jeans and a black-and-white striped shirt, he strode into the cell. A San Francisco Giants cap was pulled down low on his forehead, and he wore a pair of mirrored sunglasses.

He smiled brightly.

"So how do you like Mexico, Winn? You sure as hell found a cheap place to stay."

Cahill was so weak he could barely raise himself up to sit.

"How did you find me?" he managed to ask.

Wagner crossed the cell to him, then took off his sunglasses and slipped them into his shirt pocket. He began unwrapping the cloth around Cahill's head. Cahill looked up at him, watching his face.

"The federal marshall's office in San Diego contacted Mooney and informed him that you were being held on a stolen car beef. Apparently this DeLeon sent the feds a set of your prints. The marshall's office didn't have any trouble matching them to your prints on file at the DMV in Sacramento. Then they noticed there happened to be a warrant out for your arrest.

"That's the beauty of computers, Winn. There's no hiding from the goddamn things."

Wagner dropped the cloth onto the bunk, then carefully removed the gauze. "Jesus Christ," he sighed.

Wagner studied the eye a second longer, then replaced the gauze and wrapped the cloth back over it. He sat down on the opposite bunk. He produced a pack of cigarettes, then fished through his jeans for matches.

"They're killing me, David Earle. You've got to get me out of here."

"I know, Winn. That's why I'm here."

Wagner lit a cigarette, tossed the pack to Cahill and stood up, as if to move would help him think.

"So what's it gonna take to back this Givens off? We can't get you out of here until he drops the charges. Where can I find him?"

"He lives down the coast. Every night he shows up at a bar here called Pappagallo's."

Wagner nodded. "All right," he said. "I'll talk to him. I'll get this straightened out."

Then he turned serious. "Where's Liana?" he asked, as if her whereabouts had just occurred to him.

"I don't know," Cahill said "She might still be at the hotel," he said. "She'd be registered there under the name Joanna Douglas."

Wagner nodded without encouragement. "I'll check," he said.

Then he smiled. "Meanwhile, you stay put," he said, but Cahill couldn't find the strength to laugh.

Wagner returned the next day.

"I found a local attorney who says he knows the ropes."

Cahill watched Wagner withdraw a bottle of aspirin from his pocket and hand the bottle to Cahill. "Here," he said.

Then he sat down on the bunk. "His name is Anthony Muñoz," Wagner said. "He's got an office above a laundromat. I walk in and he's sitting at his desk, eating a half dozen fish tacos. The juice from the fucking tacos is running down his hands and dripping onto his shirt. Christ, I think he lives in that office—it stunk like it, anyway.

"But he knows who Givens is, and he doesn't like him, and I figured that was enough."

Cahill shook four of the aspirin caplets into the palm of his hand, then looked up.

"Was she there?" he asked, and immediately he realized Wagner hadn't bothered to check.

"She knows where you are, Winn. If she wants to reach you, she will."

Traveling as Joanna Douglas, she could be any-where. He guessed she'd headed down to Ensenada. From there she'd have no trouble making it down the peninsula to La Paz or Cabo San Lucas. There she could move easily among the American vacationers and *pensiones*, a worldly widow killing time in the sun.

With the charred head of a match, he scratched her initials on the wall above his bunk. He stared at the crude L.I.B.—he had all but forgotten her middle name was Ingrid, for the actress Lucky Blake said reminded him of his newborn daughter.

Cahill stared at the initials until he could see her face, her eyes, pure and blue as the Baja sky. He imagined her in a room in a hotel down the coast. She was lying down, lying in bed like he was. She was thinking of him. He knew she was.

The door at the end of the corridor opened. Cahill swung his legs over the side of his bunk and pushed up to sit. Then Wagner was grinning at him through the window in the door to his cell.

"Kneel at my feet," he declared as Hernandez let him in, his voice booming like a preacher.

Then he turned and tipped the bill of his cap to Hernandez. "And thank you so very much," he said as the cell door closed behind him.

"You found Givens?"

"Yes, I did, and he was supremely sympathetic to your situation."

Wagner tossed Cahill a pack of cigarettes, then dropped down on the opposite bunk. "He'll be down this afternoon to drop the charges."

Cahill closed his eye and took a deep breath.

"I don't believe it," he said.

"Believe it, Winn. Muñoz is greasing the wheels of justice right now." Wagner reached for the cigarettes he'd just tossed Cahill. "Givens showed up at Pappagallo's a little before midnight. Muñoz waved him over to the table and ordered up a bottle of tequila, and then I laid the situation out for him."

Wagner drew a cigarette out of the pack, then struck a match and lit it. He smiled as if pleased with himself.

"I told Givens his stolen car beef was interfering with the extradition of a man wanted for murder in the States, and that the federal marshalls in San Diego were furious. Givens got bold at first. He stood up and started thrusting his fucking cane in the air, shouting for them to come get him, but he settled down once I told him the marshalls were aware he'd put you up at his trailer for a few days. Givens was dismayed to learn they were considering bringing charges against him. I told him that at the very least they were inclined to see his disability checks got lost in the mail every month."

Cahill could imagine the blood draining out of Givens's face, the air leaking out of his bombast. He wished he'd been there.

"But then I let Givens know the marshalls' office would look favorably upon a decision to drop the car theft charges, and that I, acting as their unofficial agent, was authorized to offer him fifty bucks to facilitate the visit to DeLeon's office.

"Givens didn't have much of a choice," Wagner said. "He bitched for a few minutes, but when he stood up and swore he'd live to piss on our graves, I knew the deal was done."

It went down that afternoon.

Givens arrived at the police station and told DeLeon it had all been a misunderstanding. Initially DeLeon, who was furious that his prize prisoner was going to be taken from him, refused to accept Givens's story. Only after Cahill was tried in a Mexican court and served his time in a Mexican prison, DeLeon insisted, would he be returned to the United States.

Muñoz discretely intervened, asking to have a private word with DeLeon. They stepped out of the office for a minute. When they returned, DeLeon declared he would cooperate to the fullest extent possible.

According to Muñoz, extradition typically required a good three months to snake through the Mexican bureaucracy, but because of the condition of Cahill's eye the process was being expedited. With the car theft charges dropped, the Mexican Justice Department had no interest in Cahill; they were only too glad to declare him an undesirable alien and process him for deportation.

Muñoz guided them through the extradition process. If nothing else, he knew which officials, like DeLeon, required the *mordida* for their considerations. It infuriated Wagner, who had grown increasingly convinced that Muñoz was skimming each transaction, but he also knew they didn't have any choice. Twice he had to call Faith to wire down more money.

The day Cahill was finally to be transported to Tijuana, Wagner brought him a pair of leather *huaraches* with slabs of used car tires for soles.

"I thought you might like a souvenir of your vacation," he said.

"Where are my boots?"

"DeLeon said you came in without them."

Cahill leaned down and slipped on the *huaraches*. "That son of a bitch."

Wagner offered a weary smile. His face was thin, emaciated. Cahill knew he'd been sick ever since he arrived. He'd been living on Lomotil and painkillers.

"Listen to me, Winn," he said. "There's only one way this is going to work when we get you back to Loma Roja. You're going to have to let me deal with Stanton Douglas. You'll have to tell Douglas how it all went down. You'll have to tell him where you dumped Gillespie and what you did with the gun. You'll have to tell him Liana pulled the trigger. You can't protect her anymore. She's gone. She's gone for good. Who knows where the hell she is? If we're lucky, Douglas will let you plead out some minor charge with the stipulation that he'll urge the judge to suspend your sentence. It's the only shot you've got."

Cahill nodded tightly. He had no intention of resisting.

"You're not going to play hero again, are you, Winn?"

"Do I look like a hero?"

"You look like I feel," Wagner said.

Hernandez looked in through the window in the cell door.

"It's time," Wagner said.

They rose and walked out into the corridor. Hernandez cuffed Cahill's wrists behind his back, then knelt down and shackled his ankles.

Cahill looked at Wagner, who shrugged.

"They figure you're a risk to take off," he said.

DeLeon was standing in the doorway to his office. He smiled as they walked past.

"Perhaps someday I will go to your Las Vegas on vacation," he said. "Perhaps I will look up this pit boss who came to visit us."

Cahill stopped and turned back to him, but before he could say anything Wagner pulled him away.

Hernandez led them outside into the pitiless glare of the sun. As they stepped down from the sidewalk Cahill winced, blinded by the brilliant light. Hernandez opened the door of the police car, then shoved Cahill into the back seat.

"It's all arranged," Wagner shouted as Hernandez slammed the door. "Mooney's sending down a couple of deputies to pick you up in San Diego. You'll be home some time tomorrow morning."

Then Wagner stepped back out of the way. Cahill stared out the filthy window at him. Suddenly Wagner stiffened and stood ramrod-straight. He snapped his heels together, then slowly raised his hand and broke off a sharp military salute.

CHAPTER 23

WITH THE SIREN wailing and lights flashing, Hernandez drove up the toll road along the coast at ninety miles an hour, weaving in and out of an endless column of motor homes returning to the States. On the ruptured seat behind him, Cahill gazed out at the ocean, breathing in the air blowing in through the window.

An hour later, in Tijuana, Hernandez turned him over to officials of the Mexican Justice Department, who in turn drove Cahill to the border, where they delivered him to the federal marshalls from San Diego. It was a simple ceremony, endlessly rehearsed over the years. As the Mexicans and the federal marshalls exchanged the essential paperwork, they asked after each other's women and talked about post times at the track.

Then the marshalls drove him up to San Diego, where he spent the rest of the day in a holding cell at the county jail, waiting for Mooney's deputies.

They finally showed up at nine o'clock that

night. Cahill recognized the dour, red-faced Murdock, who had been a deputy sheriff for as long as Cahill could recall. Murdock was accompanied by a thin, pinch-faced kid named Israel. As they escorted Cahill out of the car, Israel barked out orders in a sharp, high-pitched voice. Murdock tried his best to ignore him.

They drove all night, Murdock and Israel trading shifts behind the wheel. Murdock stopped at virtually every all-night diner to fill his thermos with coffee. Israel ran on nervous energy alone. He whistled and hummed and drummed his fingers on the steering wheel, all the while maintaining a constant commentary on the local radio dispatchers.

Cahill stayed awake for as long as he could. Finally he stretched out across the seat and let sleep come over him.

At dawn he woke to Israel banging his fist on the screen between the front and back seats.

"We're here, pretty boy. Wake the fuck up."

The dark orange brick of the county jail looked cool in the morning shadows. An elderly black man in blue coveralls was sweeping the steps leading up to the main entrance. When he saw Israel and Murdock pull Cahill out of the car, he stopped and leaned back against one of the stout Roman columns that supported the building's gabled roof. The sound of the chain rattling between the shackles on Cahill's ankles seemed to unnerve him.

Drinking black coffee out of styrofoam cups, Mooney and Wagner were waiting for them in the sheriff's office. Mooney couldn't resist a smile as Cahill was led into the room.

"Well, look what the dog puked up," he said, provoking an amused titter from Israel.

He rocked forward in his chair and crushed out his cigarette in the ashtray. "Did you enjoy your stay in Mexico, Winn?"

This time Israel laughed openly.

"I've got to be honest with you, Winn—you don't look so good. Maybe you just don't travel well."

"While my client was wrongfully incarcerated," Wagner said, "he was denied proper medical treatment."

Mooney rose slowly from his chair. He crossed the office, then planted himself directly in front of Cahill.

"Is that a fact."

"Go ahead and take that cloth off," Wagner urged him. "Take a look for yourself."

"What's wrong with your eye, Winn?"

"My client needs medical attention," Wagner said. "He needs it urgently. In the absence of a medical ward in the county jail, I'm going to have to insist he be taken to Sisters of Mercy. Immediately."

Mooney laughed, then allowed himself a

smile, as if he were capable of appreciating the absurdity of it all.

"You know I almost drove down to San Diego and picked you up myself, Winn. I wish I would have. You could have told me all about the fun you had in Baja. But we'll have time for that later, won't we?"

"I'm serious," Wagner said, and Mooney turned to Murdock and Israel.

"I want one of you assholes on the door of his room twenty-four hours a day. No one goes in or out except hospital staff. He gets no visitors. He goes nowhere, not even to the can without you tagging along."

"Careful now," Wagner said, rising from his chair and inserting himself between Cahill and Mooney.

"You're beginning to step on my client's rights. You don't want me to lay any civil paper on you and your fine officers here, do you?"

"Get him out of here," Mooney hissed.

Cahill rolled his head to the left, toward the door. In her crisp white nurse's uniform, Faith quietly slipped into his room, a finger across her lips to silence him. Then she leaned back against the door and smiled at him. Her eyes watered over.

She shook her head and quickly wiped her eyes. "Oh, look at me," she said. "Here I am crying like a schoolgirl."

"Don't tell me you're back at work," Cahill said.

She shook her head, then ran her hands over her thighs, smoothing her white pants. "David Earle told me it was the only way to get in to see you."

Cahill motioned for her to come over to the bed. She sat down beside him, then reached up and tucked her hair behind her ears.

She took his hand in hers. "He told me what happened," she said. "He told me Liana's still down there."

She laughed softly to herself. "We had ourselves a time picking out names for you both. We stopped by the Blue Orchid on the way to the courthouse. Liana said she had to have a drink before she could go picking through the death certificates. I think we each had four or five shots of tequila."

He watched her long, thin fingers clutching his.

"She loved you, Winn. She truly did."

Then she rose from the bed and walked over to the window.

"I talked with Dr. Riles," she said.

She drew back the blinds and stood in the midday sun and gazed out the window as if she couldn't bear to face him, as if she needed to take a cool, professional step back.

"He told me they fractured the orbit, the bone that forms your eye socket, when they kicked you. The edema compromised the vascular supply to the retinal nerve. Finally the swelling killed the nerve."

"It's not so bad," he said, as if she were the one who needed comforting.

She turned back to him. "There's nothing can be done," she said.

"I think I'm going to wear an eyepatch."

She smiled. "Some women find eyepatches irresistible," she said.

"I'm counting on that."

She returned to the bed and sat down with him.

"What are you going to do?" she asked him. "You're not going anywhere right away, are you? Promise me you're gonna stick around for a while. I know," she said suddenly. "When you get out of here, I'll make you a huge breakfast. I'll make pancakes and fried eggs. I'll buy some real maple syrup. Do you remember how Francis Robert used to make breakfast for us on Sunday mornings?"

Cahill nodded. "Sure, I remember."

She laughed and then brushed the tears out of the corners of her eyes. "That old son of a bitch really thought he could cook, didn't he?"

Cahill reached out to her. She lay down beside him. He could feel her trembling as he held her.

He slept all the rest of the day and through the night. He still couldn't hold any food down. From a bottle suspended beside the bed, a clear solution dripped into the tube that tapped his left arm.

A nurse named Margaret bathed him with a washcloth as soon as he woke the next morning. She was a stocky woman with a heavy chest and deep folds of flesh beneath her chin. Her strong hands moved him around the bed easily; she scrubbed his skin so hard it stung.

Dr. Riles came in as she was changing the dressing on his eye.

"There will be some scarring," he said.

"Let me see."

"I think it might be best to wait."

"It's my face," Cahill snapped. "I want to see it."

The nurse recoiled, then glanced up at Riles. He nodded. She stepped out of the room for a second, then returned with a hand mirror. She held it up in front of him.

He reached up and caught her by the wrist before she could pull it away. Still nearly swollen over, his eye didn't react at all to its first glimpse of itself. Its feeble beam angled past him. A thick, purple scar ran across the ridge of his shaved brow. The skin around the socket was raised and blackened.

He slapped the mirror out of her hands. It flew across the bed and shattered on the floor. She backed away from him as if afraid he might come after her.

"That was hardly necessary," the doctor said, writing in Cahill's chart.

"So tell me what you're going to do."

"Right now you need your rest," he said.

"That's it? You think rest is going to fix this?" Cahill demanded, pointing to his own face.

"It will take time," the doctor conceded without looking up.

"Look at me!" Cahill shouted.

The doctor lifted his eyes to him. He didn't flinch. Then he slipped his pen into the pocket of his white coat and turned to leave with the nurse, who was standing by the door.

"I'll stop back in tomorrow," he said.

He tried to watch television, but he couldn't stand the leering, blue-shadowed faces. The surreal laughter drove him out of his mind.

He fell asleep. When he woke that afternoon, the nurse was standing over him, extending a small paper cup with a green-and-yellow capsule at the bottom.

"We don't want you to hurt yourself," she said.

Wagner stood behind her, watching. He nodded encouragingly.

"Doctor's orders," she said.

Cahill took the cup and flipped the capsule into his mouth.

"That's my boy," she said, and then Cahill turned his head and spat the capsule onto the floor.

Unfazed, she laughed through her nose, curling her lip.

Wagner interceded. "Why don't you give me another of those," Wagner said. "I'll see that he takes it."

The nurse glared at Cahill a second longer, then spun away. "I'll be right back," she vowed as she started toward the door.

As soon as the door swung shut, Wagner sat down on the edge of the bed.

"How are you doing?"

"How do I look?"

"You're as ugly as a dog's ass, Winn, which is to say vastly improved."

Cahill didn't laugh.

"Listen to me, Winn. The D.A. agreed to take your deposition right here. I checked with Riles, and he said it's up to you."

"Just get it over with," Cahill said.

"I thought you'd say that."

Then the door swung back into the room, and the nurse stormed through. Wagner took the paper cup from her.

"He's a little upset," he said to her. "But I think he'll be fine."

Wagner watched her leave, then turned back to Cahill and grinned broadly. "She likes you, Winn. She really does. Don't you think?"

Stanton Douglas sat in a chair beside the bed. His domed forehead was as bright and pink as if he'd been boiled. A line of sweat glistened on his upper lip.

"You contend that Mr. Gillespie threatened

you with physical harm," he said. "Then what happened?"

Cahill stared past him, into the haze of fluorescent light. It all seemed so remote, so removed, so far across the dark galaxy of memory, and yet he remembered it perfectly. He could hear the shot, the concussion thundering off the walls; he could see her staggering back, tossing the .38 onto the bed; he could see Tommy collapsing to the floor.

He tried to swallow, but his mouth was suddenly dry, his throat so constricted he could barely breathe. Then what happened? He wanted to laugh.

He could feel Wagner's hand on his arm; he jerked it away. He took a deep breath, then another, until he felt himself sinking into a pure, remorseless calm.

"She shot him," he said.

Across the room, Mooney abruptly pushed up out of his chair. "What's he talking about?"

Blood flooding into his face, Douglas turned around to the sheriff.

"What the fuck do you mean, she shot him?" Mooney demanded.

"I said she shot him!" Cahill shouted. "She shot the son of a bitch!"

"Jesus Christ," Mooney groaned. He spun away from the bed.

"It's the truth," Wagner said.

"It's a scam!" Mooney shouted.

His hands trembling, Douglas nudged his

glasses back up to the bridge of his nose, then turned to Cahill.

"For the record," he said, his voice threatening to break. "To whom are you referring?"

Cahill's hand flew up and seized Douglas's black tie; he jerked the D.A. down until they were face to face.

"Who the fuck do you think?" he shouted. "Liana! Liana!"

CHAPTER 24

HE REMAINED AT Sisters of Mercy for three more days. There was nothing more they could do for his eye. There was no hope of regaining his sight in it. Eventually the wound around it would heal, but that was all they could promise.

Faith had fashioned an eyepatch for him from soft black leather. He was wearing it when Wagner picked him up. As they pushed out of the air-conditioned hospital, the valley heat rushed up into his face like a flash of fever. He reached out and caught Wagner's arm, then paused for a second to catch his breath. Then they started for the car.

Suddenly Wagner laughed.

"I saw Mooney down at the courthouse today," he said, and then he laughed again.

"It's tearing him up, Winn. The poor bastard still thinks Liana killed Michael. Now he hears you testify that she shot Tommy. As far as Mooney's concerned, she got away from him once before—now she's done it to him again."

Cahill took a deep breath. "Fuck Mooney," was all he could think to say.

"He wants her, Winn. He wants her bad."

They drove across town—past the Madison Hotel and the park where old men sat on wooden benches in the shade, sipping beer out of quart bottles sheathed in paper bags, past the Rescue Mission and the old movie theater with its marquee advertising Spanish films to be shown on the weekend, past the Blue Orchid.

Then they pulled up in front of the old man's house.

"At least you made some damn fine news," Wagner said.

He handed Cahill a two-day-old newspaper.

"I saved you a copy for your scrapbook."

Across the top of the front page, the headline was as lurid as it was inaccurate: BIZARRE CONFESSION IN GILLESPIE MURDER. There was a photograph of Mooney standing on the railroad trestle as what remained of Tommy's body was recovered from the Edison Canal. Below were shots of him and Liana, taken from their high school yearbook. Liana had scarcely changed. He barely recognized himself.

"It's over. That's the main thing," Wagner said.

Cahill pushed out of the car. Wagner got out the other side and leaned onto the roof.

"What about the ranch?" Cahill asked.

"She sold it to the land company. They've

been wanting to buy that ranch for years. It took all of one five-minute telephone call to make the deal. It wouldn't have taken that long if Liana hadn't insisted on a few rather unorthodox terms."

Cahill turned to Wagner. "Like what?"

"Like twenty grand, in cash, that day. As soon as escrow closes, the rest of the money is automatically deposited in an account in a bank in the Netherlands Antilles. It'll get washed through a series of paper corporations all formed in the name of Joanna Douglas, then Liana can discretely move it back into the States where she can get at it."

"You set all this up?" Cahill asked.

"I'm not bad, am I?"

Cahill stared at him.

"I thought I was doing it for you, too, Winn. I thought you'd both be living off that money."

With the swamp cooler on, he lay on the sofa and fell in and out of sleep all evening and night. He was still weak. It required all his strength just to sit up. Even then he felt faint and slightly giddy, but at least the headaches had begun to dissipate.

Faith came over in the morning with a bag of groceries. "I told you I was gonna make breakfast," she said as she set the bag down on the kitchen table. "And I meant it."

She reached into the bag and withdrew a bottle of maple syrup and held it up for him to see. "You thought I'd forget the real maple syrup, didn't you?"

Cahill sat down at the table and watched her work. The kitchen was not her natural element, but she gamely set about preparing griddle cakes while strips of bacon hissed and spat in a frying pan. In a saucepan of boiling water, she heated the syrup, then poured it over the griddle cakes she'd stacked on their plates. It was the first solid food he'd risked since Mexico.

Afterward they carried their coffee out onto the front porch and sat on the steps. In the sun, Faith rolled her pants up above her knees.

"Do you hate her?" she asked, but before he could say anything, a sharp laugh escaped him.

"I know, I know," she said, yielding to a thin, joyless smile. "Do you know what Michael did to her once?"

Cahill leaned back against the step. "No."

"He'd been out drinking—I don't remember why or what about—but he came home mean. Liana told him to leave her alone, but that only made him madder. When she tried to leave, he grabbed her and threw her to the floor and started choking her. He strangled her until finally she passed out."

Faith raised her eyes to him. "And then he just left her there. He didn't know whether she was dead or alive. He just drove on out to the river to see Melissa."

She sipped at her coffee, then set the cup

back down. "I could barely understand her when she called. She could barely talk. When I got there, I was afraid he'd fractured her larynx, but she wouldn't let me call an ambulance or take her in to Sisters of Mercy because she knew the hospital would have to report it to the sheriff, and she was afraid of what Michael would do to her then.

"For days you could see where he'd dug his fingers into her neck. The bruises were black and deep, as clear as fingerprints. She wouldn't go into town until they cleared up. She was afraid to let anyone see what he'd done to her."

Faith laughed sadly. "She didn't know what to do. She was terrified of him. I told her she could stay with us. I told her to divorce the son of a bitch. David Earle said he could get a court order to keep Michael away from her, but she knew he wouldn't pay any mind to it. She was afraid he'd kill her."

She stretched her legs out into the sun.

"You can imagine how it broke her heart when Michael shot himself."

He sat on the edge of the tub while Faith changed the dressing under his eyepatch.

"How long had she been seeing Tommy?" he asked her.

"I don't know," she said.

"Weeks, months—years?"

She shrugged. "Tommy was the one who told her about Michael and Melissa," she said.

"Tommy knew Melissa; he probably knew every slut in the county.

"I suppose Liana must have started seeing him after Michael died."

"That was two years ago," he said.

Faith thought for a second. "Has it been that long?"

He borrowed Faith's car and drove out the Midway to the Harris ranch, where Cassidy's pickup was parked out at the corral behind the house. He pulled the Falcon alongside the pickup. As he climbed out of the car, he could hear Cassidy inside the sun-bleached stable.

Sonny was running circles in the corral. Cahill draped his arms over the top rail of the fence and watched the palomino run until Cassidy emerged from the stable with a thick slab of hay.

Cassidy stopped when he saw Cahill, then he heaved the hay into the corral. Furiously shaking its head, the palomino danced back out of the way as it tumbled across the ground.

"What's wrong with Sonny?" Cahill asked as Cassidy approached him.

"There's nothing wrong with him," Cassidy said.

"He looks nervous."

Cassidy studied the palomino for a moment, then turned back to Cahill. "What does a horse have to get nervous about?"

Cahill shrugged. "Liana liked to say he was a little high-strung."

"Is that right," Cassidy said flatly.

He took his handkerchief from his shirt pocket and lifted his glasses off to wipe the perspiration from the gullies beneath his eyes.

"I read about you," he said. "It seems I was right about your criminal inclinations."

"Not quite right."

He put his glasses back on, wrapping the wire frames around his ears.

"You look a little worse for the wear."

"I'm gonna make it," Cahill said.

"Of course now I'm trying to figure out why you're here."

Cahill nodded, then smiled agreeably.

"I came out so you could tell me why you bought that .38 for Liana."

Cassidy stiffened, and Cahill knew instantly that it was true. Liana never would have bought the gun herself. In the wake of Michael's death, it would have ignited too many rumors. Faith hadn't bought it for her. Neither had Wagner. There was no one else she could have turned to besides Cassidy, who knew he had already given himself away.

"She was afraid, living out here alone," he said, his voice even, rational. "She asked me to buy a handgun for her personal safety, so I did. I demonstrated its use to her. As foreman of the ranch, I considered it a function of my job."

Cahill hiked a leg up onto the bottom rail of the fence.

"Did you consider it a function of your job to tell Mooney you saw Liana running back to the house the day Michael died?"

Unfazed, Cassidy stared at him. "I was driving in from the back of the ranch when I heard the shot. Liana was right here. I saw her running toward the house."

"Lillian Harris claimed you were lying. She said you were lying to protect her."

"Lillian was wrong," Cassidy snapped. "Lillian Harris was wrong about most things."

Cahill watched as Cassidy mopped his neck with the handkerchief.

"But you were protecting her."

Cassidy turned and looked across the corral. The palomino, its head cocked, seemed to be watching them both, its tail whipping its tan haunches.

"Michael didn't kill himself," Cahill said. "It wasn't any suicide. It wasn't any accident, either. Somebody shot him. It could have been you, Cassidy."

"Well, it wasn't."

"You loved her. You knew what Michael did to her, and you hated him for it."

"I hated Michael Harris, but I didn't kill him," he said, and Cahill knew he was telling the truth.

"Then it was Tommy," Cahill said, and Cassidy didn't dispute him.

"Why didn't you ever tell this to Mooney?"

Cassidy turned to him, as if there were no one left to protect but himself.

"She wouldn't let me. She didn't want me to say anything. She said Tommy told her he'd tell Mooney that it was all her idea—that she hired him to do it."

"Did you see Tommy out here?"

"I saw his truck heading back out to the Midway."

Cahill shook his head. Suddenly he felt very tired. "Jesus," was all he could say.

CHAPTER 25

WITH ALL THE urgency of a divine revelation, it came to him on the Midway heading back into town. She was in New Orleans. That's where she said she wanted to go. That's where she had to be.

That night Wagner helped him get the old man's Pontiac running. They borrowed an air compressor to fill the tires, then jacked the car down from the blocks it had been sitting on in the garage behind the house. They installed a new battery, replaced the sparkplugs, poured a gallon of premium into the tank. Then Wagner slipped behind the wheel while Cahill sprayed ether into the carburetor, and in a great black cloud of exhaust, the engine roared to life.

He told Wagner he had to get back to Los Angeles to take care of some business there. If Wagner didn't believe him, he never let on, except to remind him that he was due back in court in five weeks.

The next morning, with three hundred dollars borrowed from Faith, he hit the road. For the first time in longer than he could remember, he knew where he was going. It made him nervous. He wasn't accustomed to such a clear sense of purpose or destination.

The trip took three days. In Las Vegas he hit a two-hundred-dollar jackpot in a quarter slot in a bar off the Strip. Outside Flagstaff he picked up a willowy blond hitchhiker named Luanne who had some good Mexican pot and a bag of amphetamines; before she got out in Dallas, she even took a few hours behind the wheel. The Pontiac broke down only once, in Beaumont, but he found another water pump in a salvage yard and was back on the road in just a couple hours.

He tried to spend the first night in New Orleans as he'd spent the two nights on the road—stretched out across the back seat—but he couldn't sleep in the suffocating heat. He bought a quart of beer and a bag of ice and then drove out to Lake Pontchartrain and sat on the seawall, but the breeze he hoped might lift off the water never materialized. He could barely breathe the hot, liquid air. As he watched the traffic roll across the causeway, he sucked on the ice until the pieces dissolved in his mouth. There was nothing he could do but slowly drink the beer and wait for the day to break.

The next day he rented a room off Constance Street in the Irish Channel district along the river. It was an old, unpainted house nearly hidden from the street by a wall of oleander and banana plants. Sheets of plaster were flaking off the red brick columns in front of the house. Wisteria grew down from the clogged, sagging rain gutters.

He parked on the street, then walked up to the house. The front door had been blue once. There were heel marks all around the handle.

A huge black woman answered. She had a bright pink mouth and rheumy eyes; her skin gleamed as if it had been oiled. Stained with blood, a white apron was tied around her waist. Dark stockings were rolled halfway up her thick calves. On the telephone she'd said her name was Ida.

"I called about the room," he said, as if to explain himself, but she didn't pay him any mind as she stepped out of the house to take a look at him.

"What you do to that eye?"

Cahill reached up to his eyepatch. "An old war injury," he said.

"Oh yeah, it is," she said, moving around to the side of him, as if to study his face from another angle. "Lord Almighty, a one-eyed white boy."

"I can pay a week's rent in advance."

She stepped back and looked up at him.

"Cash money?"

"That's right," he said.

He followed her into the house. The room

was small with flowered curtains drawn over the lone window. There was an iron-frame bed and a bureau with brass pulls. Cracks branched through the stained gray walls.

He crossed the room to the window, then turned on the fan on the sill. As he stood in front of it, he pulled the curtains back and gazed out into the back yard. There was nothing there but an old rabbit hutch slumping into the waist-high grass.

"I'll take it," he said.

He gave her the money—two moist twenty-dollar bills for a week—then returned to the Pontiac to get his suitcase out of the trunk.

Back in the room, as he began putting his clothes away, he glimpsed himself in the oval mirror on the wall above the bureau. His lips were cracked and raw. Deprived of any solid rest, his eye was red and swollen. His stubbled skin looked starved back against his cheekbones.

He ran a hand over his mouth and thought about growing his moustache back. He hadn't worn one since he and Liana lived on Kingdom Road. It had been her idea. She'd said it made him look older, harder. He'd shaved it off when he got to Los Angeles. Maybe the time had come to try it again.

He reached into the suitcase and took a photograph of her from the inside pocket. In blue jeans, a white shirt and black boots, Liana was standing in line to ride the Ferris wheel at the county fair, laughing as she bit at a tuft of cotton candy spun up onto a paper cone. Faith had taken the photograph. Before he'd left, he'd asked her if he could have it, and of course she'd given it to him though she wasn't sure why exactly he wanted it.

He was tucking the picture into the mirror frame when Ida stepped back into the room behind him. She was carrying a pitcher of water and a porcelain wash basin. A frayed yellow towel was draped over her arm.

She set the pitcher and wash basin on top of the bureau and then hung the towel over the frame at the foot of the bed. Then she paused to regard the photograph.

"You down to New Orleans to fetch her back?"

"Not exactly," he said.

He slept all day and into the night. He finally woke to the distant slam of a door.

He got up and washed his face and moved over to the fan in the window. The instant he dried himself off, sweat began trickling down his neck again, sliding across his ribs.

He pulled back the curtains. It had rained while he'd been asleep. The ground steamed; it looked like the earth itself was on fire. He could hear church bells, then the deep, unsettling fugue of ships on the river.

She was out there, somewhere close. He could feel her.

* * *

The river was high the next morning. As he drove out River Road, he could see a pair of barges working against the tireless current. The sky was the color of ash. The air surging through the open window offered little relief from the unrelenting heat.

He'd stopped at a gas station to use the public telephone. The information operator had had no listing for Liana Harris or Joanna Douglas. There was a J. Douglas, but it turned out to be a widow whose husband Jameson had died six years ago.

He tried to figure out where he was. He'd passed the Huey P. Long Bridge, then the three blue water towers. The man on the telephone had said to look for a black horse carriage on the left side of the road.

Not quite two miles further upriver he spotted the carriage and turned in beneath the arch that marked the entrance to the Jefferson Stables. He followed the muddy, puddled road past a long row of red stalls, where an elderly black man was walking a dark brown mare out to one of the barns at the base of the levee, then past the lush green paddock enclosed by a white plank fence and shaded by a huge moss-draped oak.

He pulled up in front of the stable office, then let himself in. Seated at a desk was a thick-set man in a white sweat-soaked shirt with sleeves rolled up above the elbows. His khakis were supported by red suspenders, the cuffs bunched up at the tops of his boots. On the wall above him was a photograph of an immaculately groomed black stallion on a manicured lawn. A white ribbon was taped to the picture's gilded frame.

As Cahill closed the door, the man raised his heavy frame from behind the desk and thrust out his hand. His eyes were set slightly too close together. An unlit cigar resided in the corner of his mouth.

"Rondall Chenier," he said. "I got stalls to rent at two-fifty a month. That's two feedings a day. Grain and hay. I got a boy come around every evening and comb 'em down."

"I'm not looking to rent a stall."

Chenier's broad face abruptly darkened.

"I'm looking to find an old friend." Cahill took the photograph of Liana out of his pocket and handed it to Chenier. "You seen her around?"

Chenier studied it a second, then dropped back into the chair behind his desk. He kicked his boots up onto the typewriter leaf.

"This filly got a name?"

"Joanna Douglas," Cahill said. "Or maybe Liana Harris."

Chenier looked up. "She got two names?"

"She goes by either one."

"My, my."

"It's kind of complicated."

"Oh yes," he said. "Oh yes, it is. I'll bet it's complicated."

Cahill picked up a pencil and scribbled his name on a slip of paper, then added the telephone number at the boarding house. He took the snapshot back from Chenier.

"If she comes around, give me a call. It's worth a hundred bucks to you."

Chenier whistled at him.

"She must have done you bad."

He spent the rest of the day checking out the other stables along River Road. On the way back into the city, he stopped at a place along the river called Major's to get something to eat. The bartender had wild red hair scorched back at the temples and a face the color of a sore. He kept a cocked silver-plated Colt .45 on top of the cash register.

Cahill sat down at a table covered with newspaper. A waitress with long black hair teased up at the back of her head tore off the top sheet of paper. Her heavy chest swung from side to side beneath a nearly translucent T-shirt as she set a plate of rice and red beans and boiled shrimp in front of him. It was the daily special, the only item posted on the chalkboard beside the door to the kitchen. Then she brought him a pitcher of beer to dilute the cayenne pepper.

No one had recognized Liana at any of the stables. It didn't surprise him. It didn't discourage him, either. She loved horses. There were times when he believed she loved horses more than people. Someday she'd go for a ride. It was his only chance.

Tomorrow he'd head up into Mississippi. Less than an hour away, near Picayune, there were more stables. It was going to take time, he knew that much. But he'd find her. He knew he would.

CHAPTER 26

IT TOOK NEARLY five weeks.

He was in his room, lying on the bed when Ida pounded once on the door and then let herself in.

"Man named Chenier call and say you owe him money."

Cahill leapt up off the bed, then shoved past her toward the door.

"He ain't the only one," she shouted after him.

Chenier was sitting in the stable office with his boots kicked up onto his desk, burning holes in the newspaper with his cigar.

"You saw her?" Cahill asked.

Chenier smiled, the cigar rolling across his purpled lips. "And a pleasure it was. My, my. She's a looker, ain't she?

"She came out yesterday afternoon and took herself a ride. She rode up onto the levee, was gone so long I thought she was up to Baton Rouge."

The ash dropped from Chenier's cigar and landed on his shirt; he swatted it off.

"Of course the minute I saw her, I couldn't help but wonder what a woman like her might see in a man such as yourself."

"Where is she?" Cahill asked him.

"Don't you fret none," Chenier said, patting his shirt pocket. "I got her address right here.

"Of course I have to tell you the value of this information has gone up some since we last talked. I mean, where else you gonna get this information but from ol' Rondall here?"

Chenier smiled at him.

"Now what if I was to have myself a conversation with Miss Joanna Douglas, and what if I was to tell her this one-eyed man come around asking after her?"

Chenier took his feet off the desk, then rocked forward in his chair.

"See, I think maybe she don't want you to know where she is—and I do believe she could afford my strictest confidence."

Cahill lunged across the desk and threw his forearm into Chenier's neck. Chenier's head smashed back into the photograph on the wall behind him. The glass rained down onto his shoulder. The cigar tumbled out of his mouth. Chenier pushed up from the desk, but before he could raise his hands, Cahill delivered another blow to his stomach. Doubled over, Chenier gasped for air. Cahill slammed his face down hard on the desk.

He knew Chenier was through; he could see his legs give out beneath him. A voice in the back of his head screamed for him to stop, but he couldn't help himself. He picked Chenier's head off the desk, then ran him headlong into the wall. With a dull crack, the wallboard caved in, and Chenier collapsed to the floor. Then he lay still.

Cahill's heart pounded in his chest. It took all his strength to release his clenched fists. He took a deep breath and wiped his face on his shirt. Then he knelt down beside Chenier and rolled him onto his back and ripped Liana's address out of his shirt pocket.

She lived near the Garden District, just uptown from Lee Circle. With Doric columns across the porch and shuttered dormer windows lining the slate roof, it was an elegant, dignified house, carefully restored to the luxury and splendor of the genteel homes that flanked it. Behind the ornate wrought-iron fence, date palms lined the walk leading up to the house. The gardens lay in shadow beneath two ancient magnolias. A gleaming white Porsche was parked in the driveway.

From down the street, slumped behind the wheel of the Pontiac, it looked to Cahill like it suited Liana fine. He wouldn't have expected anything less.

* * *

He watched the house all afternoon and evening. He didn't see her until that evening when a black Mercedes pulled in behind the Porsche. A tall, middle-aged man in a white suit slid out from behind the wheel and carried a bouquet of white roses up to the front porch. With his silver hair and practiced smile, he looked as bright and cool as a newly minted dime.

He disappeared into the house. A few minutes later, they came out together. Her long blue dress drew tight around her waist but sailed freely out from around her legs as they walked out to the Mercedes. Her arm was slipped through his. Beneath the broad white brim of the hat Faith had given her to take to Mexico, she was laughing.

Cahill watched him open the door for her; he watched her lift her legs into the car. As the Mercedes backed out onto the street and then drove away, he realized the last time he'd seen her, she was fleeing into the barrio. It seemed like a lifetime had passed since then—his in jail and the hospital, hers here, attended by handsome callers. It made him hate her all the more.

He followed them down to Galatoire's in the old French Quarter. While they ate, he smashed in one of the Mercedes' windows and then quickly rifled through the glovebox. From the registration slip, he learned the man was Dr. Etienne Killy, and that, too, seemed perfect.

In a doorway across the street, he waited for them to return. When Killy discovered that his

Mercedes had been broken into, he flew into an emasculated rage. That such a vulgar and apparently casual crime could have been committed against him was more than he could bear. It was all Cahill could do not to laugh.

They returned to the house, and Liana invited Killy inside, but she turned him back out shortly after midnight. From down the street, Cahill watched Killy drive off. Later, he thought, he'd look the doctor up and fix the Mercedes proper.

Then he waited. He waited until all the neighboring houses fell dark, then he climbed out of the Pontiac, hurdled the wrought-iron fence and then stole along the side of the house to the trellis-covered patio in back. The double glass doors to the parlor were unlocked. He slipped quietly inside.

Liana was upstairs. She had to be. Those were the last lights extinguished. The hardwood floor groaned beneath him as he crossed the parlor floor to the stairs. He took them slowly, two at a time.

At the landing at the top of the stairs, the door to her bedroom was slightly ajar. In the faint light filtering through the window from the streetlamps, he could see her on the bed. Beneath the broad blades of the ceiling fan, she quietly moaned, then rolled onto her back. He held his breath, afraid she might wake, afraid she wasn't asleep at all.

Finally she was still again, and he gently pushed the door back.

Then he was upon her. He clamped a hand over her mouth, pinned her shoulders down with his knees. She woke in a dead panic, but he smothered her scream and wouldn't let her break away.

With his free hand, he groped toward the nightstand, nearly knocking the lamp over before reaching up under its shade. The sudden burst of light blinded them both. She flinched, as if expecting to be struck, but then she recognized him.

Tears streamed down her face. Her chest heaved from the struggle. Slowly he lifted his hand from her mouth. She didn't try to scream. All she could do was sob.

"You made it," she cried. "I knew you would."

He pushed off her. She rose with him and threw her arms around his neck.

"I prayed you'd come. I prayed you'd know to look for me here. I've been waiting for weeks."

Then she pulled back out of his arms to look at him. She ran her hands through his hair, then gently touched the patch over his eye.

"Oh, look at you, baby. What did they do to you?"

She fell against him again, wrapping her arms around him, pressing her head against his shoulder.

"I knew they were hurting you. I saw them kicking you, but I couldn't stop. I couldn't go back for you. There was nothing I could do."

Abruptly Cahill pulled away from her and stood up.

"What's wrong?" she asked, suddenly alarmed.

He walked over to the window and gazed out at the street. It had begun to rain.

"How did you get out of Mexico?"

"I hid," she said. "I hid in this little shack, and then that night this old man came in. He knew what had happened; he knew they were looking for me, but he let me stay. I hid there all night. I couldn't sleep. I just sat there and looked out the window, thinking any minute the police would pull up and arrest me.

"Then the next morning, I gave him fifty dollars to drive me down to Ensenada, where I caught a bus down to Cabo San Lucas. It took forever, but finally we got there. I stayed only a few days before I caught a flight to the mainland and then came up here."

Cahill couldn't help but laugh; he knew it would have been that easy for her.

"What?" she wanted to know, as if afraid he didn't believe her.

He turned back to her. "I know about Michael," he said.

She seemed startled, caught off guard. "What about Michael?"

"I know what he did to you."

She stared emptily at him.

"I know about Tommy, too. I know he killed Michael. I know he did it for you."

"That's not true," she protested, but he wasn't listening to her.

"The only problem was then you couldn't get rid of Tommy. You couldn't threaten him. You couldn't pay him off. Once you got rid of Michael, you couldn't get away from Tommy."

He shook his head.

"Then I rolled into town."

He laughed. "It was perfect. It was brilliant. You knew I'd come out to the ranch. You knew Tommy would come back and find us."

"That's not true!"

"You knew I wouldn't call the sheriff after you shot him, just like you knew I'd be the one to look good for it."

"No!" she shouted.

She leapt up off the bed and rushed at him, flailing at him with her fists. He caught her by the wrists and spun her around, then he shoved her against the wall, his knee in the small of her back, his mouth on her ear, so close she couldn't even turn her head.

"I even know about the good doctor Killy," he said, and then he flung her back onto the bed.

She gathered herself up on the edge of the mattress.

"You've been watching me?"

He laughed at her.

"For how long?"

"What difference does it make?"

"If you've been watching me for long, then you know he doesn't mean anything. You know I've only seen him this one time. I never set you up," she pleaded. "You know that; you have to know that. Why else would I have met you in Rosarito? I arranged everything with David Earle, and then I rushed down to meet you, and when that blew up, I came here and waited for you."

Cahill spun back to the window.

"What else was I supposed to do? Tell me what else I should have done. I couldn't contact you. I couldn't take the risk. I got here as soon as I could. I've been waiting for you ever since."

She pushed off the bed and came up behind him. She slipped her arms around his waist and pressed her head against him.

"Don't you see?" she cried. "We're both here. This is it."

"Shut up!" he snapped.

"This is what we wanted!"

"Shut up, I said!"

He didn't want to hear it. He didn't care what she said.

He twisted away from her. He couldn't think. Nothing was simple, nothing clean. Nothing made any sense.

But why else would she have sold the ranch and then met him in Baja? She could have stayed in Loma Roja. She could have gone any-where and still collected the money from the sale of the ranch. She could have disappeared with it all. Instead, she'd gone to Rosarito, where she knew he'd find her at the old beach hotel, just like she knew he'd find her here.

It made his head ache—a sudden, sharp shaft of pain closed his eyes. He reached up and pinched the bridge of his nose, and suddenly he realized that that had been their critical mis-take: to ever have believed that they might get away with what they'd done. They were not that lucky. They were dreamers, losers, their lives driven by bad instincts, guided by wrong decisions. All they knew was to try to survive, and they weren't even very good at that.

It didn't leave him any choice. He had to be-lieve her, even after all she'd done to him. He could no more be free of her than the moon could slip the pull of the earth. Gravity, des-tiny, it made no difference now. She was all he had left.

He took a deep breath, then opened his eyes. The rain had stopped. Nothing moved in the gardens below—only the mist, trailing through the trees like smoke.

Then he noticed them, two men down the street, peering in through the windows of the Pontiac. He started to call out and warn them to leave the car alone, but then he stopped himself. There was nothing in the car. The doors weren't locked.

One of the men was black. He was heavy-set and wore a baggy gray suit. The other wore khakis and a bright blue shirt. The shoulders of his tan cloth coat were soaked through from the rain. The man in the khakis lit a cigarette, then snapped his lighter closed and slipped it into his pocket. As he looked up at the house, Cahill felt like a spike had been driven into his chest.

He looked in the other direction down the block. A dark blue sedan was parked at the corner. He tried to remember if it had been there earlier, but he couldn't be sure. There was a man behind the wheel—then no, there wasn't. His mind was running away on him.

There was no sense taking any chances. Liana was hot. After missing his court date, so was he.

He spun away from the window and pulled Liana up off the bed.

"Get dressed," he said, his voice urgent, hard. "We've got to get out of here."

She pulled her arm away, resisting him.

"What are you talking about?"

He tore the blue dress off the hanger on the back of the door and tossed it at her.

"They know we're here."

"Who?" she demanded.

"Just do it!"

She didn't move but only stared at him. He

swept her keys off the bureau, then started down the stairs.

He waited for her in the pantry off the kitchen. He peered through the curtain on the door and looked out at the Porsche. The driveway was narrow, two thin strips of concrete leading between the wrought-iron fence on the left and a white brick wall on the right. Two iron lampposts stood at the mouth of the driveway.

"I'll go first," he said to her. "I'll walk out real easy and get in the car. The instant it starts, you come out, nice and slow and relaxed."

"I know where we'll go," she said.

Her hand squeezed his. He turned away from the window.

"I've got a million ideas."

He wanted to laugh at her, but knew he couldn't, not now. "Let's get out of here first," he said.

He turned and peered back out at the Porsche. There was no way to know what was out there until he got outside. The time had come. With the ignition key in his hand, he took a deep breath, glanced back at Liana, then let himself out the door.

He closed it quietly, then started for the car. Suddenly the night that had seemed so still was alive with sound: the water still running in the gutters, rain dripping from the sycamores and magnolias, the scratch of each step on the concrete. He knew better than to risk looking down the street but couldn't resist a glance at the Pontiac. No one was near it. The two men were gone.

It seemed to take forever to reach the car. He opened the door and slipped behind the wheel, inserted the key into the ignition, turned it. The engine started instantly and fell into a steady idle.

Right on cue, the door to the pantry opened, and Liana was walking toward the car. It seemed to him then that she'd never looked so good in her life. And once they hit the street, no one was keeping up with them.

He leaned across the seat and pushed open the door for her. Suddenly the sharp, hard command came out of nowhere.

"Freeze! Police!"

She dove into the car. As he jammed it into reverse, he glanced up into the rearview mirror and saw that he'd been right: Mooney was standing in the driveway, his service revolver drawn and braced with both hands, his partner kneeling at the foot of the brick wall.

"Go!" she screamed. "Go, goddamn you!"

He dropped the clutch and stomped down on the accelerator. The tires howled on the slick pavement but then took hold. They hurtled down the driveway, scraping off the brick wall, clipping one of the lampposts, then shooting out onto the street.

He spun the wheel hard to the right, slammed on the brakes. As the Porsche swung around, he shoved it into gear. Mooney and his partner opened fire, their muzzles flashing against the night.

He floored it. Tires shrieking, they fishtailed down the street. Suddenly the windshield exploded in front of him, the shattered glass crashing into his face. He couldn't see. Then he could feel the car kicking up over the curb. Before he could hit the brakes, the Porsche plowed into the thick trunk of a sycamore. All he could hear was the long blare of the horn.

Stunned, he slowly sat back up. His face had struck the steering wheel hard. He could taste the blood in his mouth. He looked over to Liana, saw the open door. Panic closed over him. She wasn't there.

His door was wedged shut. He threw his shoulder against it and then managed to push it back. The instant he climbed out, he saw her lying in the street at the foot of the driveway, splayed out across the wet pavement. Mooney was standing over her with his revolver drawn.

''No!'' he screamed.

He started back to her, but before he could take two steps, Mooney's partner caught him from behind and slammed him face down on the street.

With his arms pulled back behind him and his wrists cuffed, he raised his head. With the tip of his black shoe, Mooney nudged Liana's left arm off her chest. Her limp hand slapped back onto the street.

"She's hurt!" he screamed at the people now streaming out of their houses. "Somebody call an ambulance!"

Then Mooney knelt down beside her. Cahill watched as he lifted her bloodied hair from her face. He studied her a moment, then stood back up, then returned his revolver to the shoulder harness under his coat.

"No!" Cahill screamed, and then he closed his eye and let his head fall back down on the asphalt.

CHAPTER 27

THE ROAD DIPPED as it ran along the edge of the walnut orchard, then swept back up onto the crest of the levee. His hands cuffed in his lap, Cahill gazed out the window at the river. On outstretched wings, a great blue heron glided across the water. He watched it settle on the shore of a wooded island, formed in the heart of a long bend in the river.

"You know what they say about New Orleans, Winn?"

Cahill turned away from the river. Mooney was driving, his elbow propped out the open window. The wind pushed back his thin hair. Through the wire mesh screen above the seat, Cahill caught his lidded eyes in the rearview mirror.

"They say on any given day you're likely to see more nuns and naked women in New Orleans than anywhere else."

Mooney turned around and looked back over his shoulder at him. "I wouldn't know if that's the truth," he said. "I never did see any of them nuns."

He smiled broadly, then turned back to the road.

"I'll tell you where you made your big mistake, Winn. The Irish Channel. The Irish Channel is a crime-infested neighborhood."

Mooney dragged on his cigarette, sucking the smoke deep into his lungs.

"Jackson just happened to be in the neighborhood on a stolen property beef, and there was Francis Robert's Pontiac, sitting there with those pretty California plates. He couldn't hardly help but notice they were five years expired. He had to run the damn things."

Mooney glanced back up into the rearview mirror. "Naturally I'd sent the plates out over the wire as soon as you failed to appear in court.

"So I'm sitting in my office one afternoon, and I get this call, and I find out the Pontiac's turned up in New Orleans, of all the goddamned places.

"Can you believe that, Winn? I don't know whether my luck is that good, or yours is just plain bad."

Mooney laughed.

"I was there ten days, thanks to you. That's how long I sat on you. I knew you'd find her. I knew you'd lead me right to her, and by God you didn't let me down."

Cahill turned and looked back out the window. They'd held him three days in New Orleans. A handful of complaints had been filed against him, but the district attorney's office had been glad to return him to California to face the charges pending against him there. Mooney, of course, had eagerly consented to escort him back. In a sealed pine casket, Liana came home on the same flight.

Faith had made all the arrangements to bury her. The cemetery was on a small rise not far from Hudson Grove. It was enclosed by eucalyptus trees, planted as wind breaks years ago, and as Mooney slowed down to turn off River Road, Cahill could see their slender, gray-green leaves turning in the breeze.

They drove up the narrow gravel road that led into the cemetery. Wings folded and head bowed, a dark marble angel knelt beside the gate. Her grieving face had been recently blasted with a shotgun. Her stone flesh was pocked and chipped from the buckshot.

Mooney parked in the shade of an ancient willow. Across the cemetery, Faith and Wagner were standing beneath a white nylon canopy raised on metal poles, sheltering the casket from the sun. Cleveland Wills, the Baptist minister Faith had hired to perform the service, was seated in a folding chair, mopping his brow with a handkerchief. Wills had never known Liana, except by reputation, of course, but for thirty-five dollars he had vowed to speak warmly of her.

Mooney climbed out of the car, then opened Cahill's door. He reached down to help Cahill out, but Cahill drew back, refusing him. Mooney laughed, then stood back out of the way as Cahill struggled to his feet.

"I'll tell you this, Winn, that David Earle's one slick son of a bitch. How he conned Judge Meacham into this furlough, I don't know. But I do know it lasts exactly one hour, and you've already burned twenty minutes.

"Then your ass is mine again."

Cahill turned to walk away, but before he could take a step, Mooney grabbed his arm.

"You're not gonna try anything stupid here, are you, Winn?"

They stared at each other for a second. Cahill gave him nothing. Then he tugged his arm out of Mooney's grasp and started across the grass.

Her eyes glittering with tears, Faith rose and kissed him on the cheek as he ducked under the sagging canopy. Wagner nodded, then clamped his hand on Cahill's shoulder. Wills rose from his chair and stood before them.

"Are we waiting for anyone else?" he asked.

Faith tried to answer but then could only manage a smile. Cahill slipped his arm around her shoulders; Wagner took her hand.

"Just get on with it," Cahill said. "This is all there is."

They lowered the casket into the rich red soil. Cahill stepped up to the edge of the grave. As he tossed the lilies in after her, he could smell the dank breath of the earth itself. His throat tightened. Soon enough the ground was going to swallow them all.

He stepped back, pulled Faith close, then looked up at the sky. He took a deep breath. A marsh hawk circled overhead, coasting on the thermals. Finally it was over. The time had come to put Liana out of his mind. He'd forget her now. He had all the time in the world. He had the rest of his life.

ABOUT THE AUTHOR

K. PATRICK CONNER is the author of *Blood Moon* and an editor and writer with the *San Francisco Chronicle*'s Sunday Magazine. He makes his home in San Francisco, California.

SPELLBINDING THRILLERS ...
TAUT SUSPENSE